EARL
of Alnwick

CHAPTER ONE

Alnwick Hall
Northumberland, England
September, 1821

KATIE PRINGLE'S SCREAM caught the attention of Niall Jameson, Earl of Alnwick, while he happened to be nakedly bathing in a side pool of the river between the boundary of their estates on this fine autumn day. The sun was shining and a gentle breeze ruffled his hair as he washed off the sweat and grime of a solid day's work rebuilding the rundown stables at Alnwick Hall. "For the love of…Katie, no!"

Niall watched in horror as the bane of his childhood existence, the Perfect Miss Pringle, caught her fancy slipper on the hem of her elegant gown, tripped, and tumbled headlong into the deepest part of the river.

He cursed as she fell in with a loud splash and was immediately caught up in the swiftly moving current that would certainly pull her down into its cold depths because the irritating girl, his childhood nemesis, did not know how to swim.

She had never learned.

For this reason, Niall knew she'd always been afraid of the river and had never dared go near it before.

So what was she doing here now?

He pushed off the bank and swam as fast as he ever had in his life toward the irritating girl, desperate to reach her before she sank beneath the surface, never to be seen again.

As often as he'd dreamed of tossing her into these swirling waters and laughing as she flailed and sputtered, her perfect pigtails and neatly tied bows coming undone, he had never considered actually having her drown.

His heart was pounding by the time he reached her side. All that remained visible was one lace-gloved hand. He firmly entwined his fingers in hers and hoisted her upward so that her head broke the surface. "Katie, of all the stupid, reckless–"

She coughed in his face.

Well, she hadn't meant to do it. She was obviously terrified and struggling to regain her breath. As he helped her, she spit out water and took in great gulps of air. "Katie, you–"

"I know. Don't yell at me."

She tearfully threw her arms around his neck and pressed herself to his body, holding him in a death grip while sobbing. "Thank you! I'm so grateful. You saved my life."

Yes, he had.

He was surprised by how good it made him feel. He'd spent most of his life avoiding responsibility, doing all for himself with little care for others. His father and grandfather before him had been cut from the same cloth, which probably explained why the Alnwick holdings were in such a dismal state.

But now that he was earl, he'd been trying to improve matters.

Katie suddenly gasped and tried to push away. "Oh, spillikins! It's you. What are you doing here, Alnwick?"

He tightened his grip on her body on the chance she was stupid enough to actually let go of him. "Fight me and I vow I shall let you drown, you little peahen. The more important question is what are you doing here? Aren't you supposed to be in London marrying into one of England's wealthiest families?"

Her wedding was supposed to have taken place a week ago. She was marrying the Marquess of Yardsley, an inconsiderate arse who was never going to be faithful to the Perfect Miss Pringle, but why should he care? Katie was an uptight, righteous–

"I ran away."

He burst out laughing. "What? Am I hearing right? You? The paragon of perfection, the obedient, never a hair out of place, never a white glove soiled, soul of propriety and decorum, is a runaway bride? Did you run off before or after the wedding ceremony?"

"Before."

He began to swim her over to the safety of his side of the river, but slowed his strokes so he could pry more information out of her. The sun was shining down on them and there was not a cloud in the sky. He'd finished his daily chores and was in no hurry to get back to an empty home. "What happened?"

"He...he was...I caught him with my best friend." He could not tell whether the water now spilling down her cheeks was from her soaked hair or whether she was crying. He hoped she was not crying.

Then he'd be forced to feel sorry for her.

"You caught him with Sybil? As in caught talking to her? So what?"

"They weren't talking. He was *with* her."

Bollocks.

He supposed it was too late to simply set her safely on the grassy bank and swim away. He was too incensed by the way she'd been treated by Yardsley, that selfish prig. Nor had he ever liked her supposed best friend. "Sybil was never to be trusted. I warned you about her."

She sniffled as she frowned at him. "And she warned me never to trust you."

"And you believed that lying witch?" He had a mind to let go of her and watch her flail for a few desperate moments before taking her back in his arms. He would have. He should have. Except her body felt surprisingly good against his and he was not eager to let her go.

"Why shouldn't I believe her? You were a terror as a child and an impossible rake as you grew older. You did nothing to improve your reputation. What was I to think?"

He tried to concentrate on their conversation and ignore the fact that she was no longer a skinny rail but had lovely, soft breasts that were now rubbing against his chest. "Even so, Sybil was no better. She was just sneakier about it."

"I learned that lesson the hard way. I caught them together in the clerestory. Yardsley did not even have the decency to wait until after the wedding to be unfaithful. He and Sybil were..." She inhaled raggedly and released the breath in a sob. "They were...cavorting...in an intimate manner in the church. *In the church.* Less than an hour before we were to marry."

"So you ran off." Her legs were entwined with his and her thigh was now rubbing against his private parts, although he was trying his best to avoid *that* contact.

Not that she realized what she was doing.

Or that he was naked.

Katie always was a naive widgeon.

In truth, it was perhaps the only thing he liked about her. Well, he'd now add her breasts to the short list of things he liked about her.

In truth, she was a good, sweet girl.

He'd been the bad one, and too much of an arse to appreciate how nice she was.

"They laughed at me when I caught them. Yes, I ran off and never looked back. They are welcome to each other for all I care."

"Good for you. That took courage. I'm proud of you."

Her eyes rounded in surprise. "Why do you say that? I thought you hated me."

They were now approaching his side of the river and he knew he'd soon have to release her. "I never hated you. Yes, you rankled me. I disliked your perfect manners and your always perfect behavior. There were often times I wanted to push you into a mud puddle just to knock you down off your pedestal."

"You did push me into a mud puddle once."

The accusation surprised him. "When? I don't ever remember doing that."

"I was fifteen and you were twenty. You showed up drunk and soaking wet to my birthday party. It had been raining hard earlier in the day so the ground was wet. You were too cobbled to find the front door, so you stumbled around to the back and passed out on a bench in our garden. I ran out to fetch you and bring you inside before you caught a lung infection and died."

He hoisted her onto a grassy patch of the bank, briefly wondering when she was going to realize he was naked and start screaming again. "Why did you run out to me? Why didn't you send a footman?"

"I didn't want you to get in trouble and thought I could sneak you in myself. But when I tried to help you up, you tumbled off the bench and took me down with you."

"Into a mud puddle?"

She nodded.

"If one were to be precise about it, I didn't push you into it then. We simply fell in because you were foolish enough to try to lift me."

"I was only trying to help. I wanted to protect you so that you would not get in trouble with your family."

He laughed. "That's rich. My family? My father and grandfather would have clapped me on the shoulder and asked me how many girls I'd…entertained that night."

Katie looked as though she was about to cry again.

"*Blast*. What's wrong now?"

"Is that what you were doing on the night of my party?"

"No, I wasn't. I was merely drinking. I'm nothing like Yardsley." Not that he was a saint, but even he would have had the decency not to cheat on his bride on his wedding day.

"My parents assured me you were worse."

"They just assumed I would be since I'm a Jameson. But Yardsley's reputation is no better. They were willing to overlook his because he is one of the richest men in England. I'm sorry they pushed you into marrying him. I could have told them it would never work. A girl like you needs to marry for love."

He started to get out of the water, but thought better of it. Katie, despite being the most irritating girl in existence, had just endured a bad scare and narrowly avoided drowning. He would take it easy on her today. "Close your eyes, Katie."

"Why?"

"Are your senses so addled that you have not noticed? I'm wearing no clothes. And by the way, that twitching thing you felt against your thigh wasn't a fish."

She shrieked and rose to scamper away, but her slippers were wet and the grass was slick. She tumbled back into the water, panicked and began to flail even though the water on this side of the river was not deep. It would have only come up to her chest had she bothered to stand.

He lifted her up and held her against him. "Katie, calm down. I'm sorry. I shouldn't have said that. Stop struggling. You're not going to drown."

She shrieked in his ear.

Which reminded him to ask why she was screaming earlier. "Was someone chasing you?"

"Not someone. Some *thing*. I accidentally walked too close to a fox den and the mother fox chased me away from her kits. I thought she was going to bite me."

He tried not to roll his eyes. "You are quite the adventuress, aren't you?"

Her bottom lip quivered. "Don't mock me. I've been ridiculed enough this week."

"Sorry. My point is, you wouldn't last more than five minutes on your own."

"I'll have you know I've lasted perfectly well since leaving London, and that was almost a week ago. I made it all the way up here on my own, didn't I?"

"I suppose. Why are you still wearing your wedding gown? And your perfect white gloves? Don't you have a wardrobe filled with clothes at Pringle Grange?"

She cleared her throat. "I do. But no one knows I'm here yet. I rode the mail coach as far as St. Michael's Priory and then walked the rest of the way. I was just cutting through your property on the way to my house when the fox chased me."

No wonder she looked pale and exhausted in addition to looking like a drowned water rat. Her long, dark hair fell flat against her cheeks. Her big, green eyes usually sparkled as bright as emeralds, but also looked rather flat at the moment. She had dark circles under her eyes. "Katie, do your parents know where you've gone?"

She cast her gaze down. "No."

"Bollocks, they'll be worried sick about you."

"I know. But I needed to get away before they made me marry Yardsley. I wanted time to decide what I'm going to do. Oh, dear! What if they have Bow Street runners waiting for me at Pringle Grange? I should have thought of it sooner."

He gently brushed back the few strands of hair plastered to her cheek. "You are too tired to think straight just now."

She nodded and began to nibble her lip.

After a moment, she looked up at him with pleading eyes. "I can't go back there until I'm certain it's safe. Would you mind terribly if I came home with you?"

"To Alnwick Hall?"

That would be a terrible mistake.

She was still looking up at him with soft, trusting eyes. "Just for a day or two."

"Out of the question. Phillipa isn't here. You and I would be alone save for the Crisps. The wife is my housekeeper and her husband takes care of the Alnwick grounds."

"I remember them. They've been with your family for ages. I would be no trouble to any of you. I'll do my best to stay quietly out of your way."

He arched an eyebrow. "You do know my reputation, don't you?"

"Are you suggesting I'm in danger of being seduced by you? I thought you didn't like me."

"I don't," he grumbled, surprised that she was not more afraid of him. In truth, she appeared intrigued more than horrified.

"Then where's the problem?"

"I suppose there isn't one." Since she did not seem at all put out by the arrangement, he lifted her back onto the river bank. "Fine. Sit here while I dress. Close your eyes and don't you dare peek."

"As if I ever would." She tipped her chin in the air. "I have no interest in gawking at you."

"Good. Then don't. Because I am completely, bare-arsed naked. Something you would have noticed if you weren't so distracted by almost dying." He swam the few strokes to the spot where he'd left his clothes spread atop a gorse bush. The low lying shrubs and small trees with branches leaning out over the water were not going to hide much of him if she did choose to look.

As for him, he did not much care if she saw him naked. But the sight of him would give the girl another shock and she'd had enough surprises this week. Not even he had the heart to cause her more strife.

He quickly donned his breeches, boots, and work shirt that still reeked of his sweat. "Mrs. Crisp will feed us," he called over his shoulder as he tucked in his shirt. "She's an excellent cook. I'm sure you're hungry."

"I am."

He strode out from behind the barrier of shrubs and took the reins of his trusted gray, Templar, who was tethered nearby. "She's a much better cook than your Mrs. Simms at Pringle Grange. Her food tastes like sawdust. Why does your mother keep her on?"

"Her cooking is just fine. But I will agree your Mrs. Crisp is unrivaled."

He returned to her side, wondering why she was suddenly blushing. Had she been peeking? No, the Perfect Miss Pringle would never do such a thing. "I'm sure there will be a hearty stew waiting for us. But you'll have to change out of those wet clothes first. Phillipa keeps some gowns here. We'll find you something of hers to wear."

"I would appreciate that."

"Mrs. Crisp will help you out of your wedding gown." Because he certainly had no desire to put his hands on her to help her out of her clothes.

"Don't call it that."

"What? Your wedding gown? As you wish. It's ruined anyway." The fine silk was soaking wet and molded to her body.

Her very shapely and beautiful body.

Blessed saints!

When did this happen?

He picked her up, ignoring the jolt of heat now coursing through him as he took her back in his arms to seat her on Templar. "Hold onto the saddle or Templar's mane. I'll walk you back."

"No. I don't want anyone to see me. Get on behind me and take me back to your home as fast as possible."

Bad idea.

He shrugged. "All right."

"Thank you, Alnwick."

"Call me Niall. I hate that title."

"Why?"

"Because it came with nothing but a pile of debts and an estate on the verge of turning to rubble." He climbed up behind her and wrapped his arms around her, telling himself it was only to keep her from falling off.

It had nothing to do with the fact that perhaps...just perhaps...her body was magnificent and felt extraordinarily good against him.

This was Katie Pringle.

His lifelong nemesis.

He was never going to admit that he might have been wrong about her all these years.

No, he and Katie did not like each other.

He was going to keep it that way.

Even if his body disagreed.

CHAPTER TWO

K ATIE DID NOT trust Niall Jameson, Earl of Alnwick.
  She never had.

Oh, he'd been nice to her today and quite valiant in rescuing her. But he was still a womanizing, rakehell cad, and she could never, ever let down her guard around him. Nor could she ever let him know that she had peeked while he was dressing.

She couldn't help it.

Curiosity got the better of her.

And now that she'd seen all of him, her treacherous her heart was still in palpitations. Who knew a man could be so finely shaped?

She hadn't expected his body to look better than those on the marble statues depicting the gods of Olympus one found in museums. She knew he had a handsome face. He'd always been sinfully handsome. But his body had filled out incredibly well. Spectacularly, now that she'd seen all of him.

And by all, she meant *all*.

Front, back, legs, chest, and all parts inbetween. Gawked, ogled, and noticed with heart pounding clarity.

He had long legs, a trim waist, and muscles piled on muscles that were attached to fascinatingly broad shoulders and firm arms. "Do you think the Crisps will let on that I am here?"

"No, Katie. They've always liked you. They can be trusted."

She leaned her head against his shoulder and closed her eyes, intending to rest them for just a moment. There was something quite reassuring about the resonant depth of his voice and the protective way he held her in his arms.

She'd often dreamed of being held in his arms, but never imagined it would ever happen. He didn't like her.

She didn't really like him, either.

Yet, she'd always been drawn to him. Infatuated, she supposed.

And he'd always rebuffed her.

She shook out of the thought, not wanting it to mar this perfect moment. The day was perfection as well. A gentle breeze blew in from the North Sea, carrying the scent of salt water inland with it. The sun was shining brightly, and the scent of grass, pine leaves, and roses also filled the air. It was so much nicer than the London air and the scents emanating off the Thames.

"How are you holding up, Katie?" he asked as Templar loped across the meadow toward Alnwick Hall.

"I'll be all right. My heart is beginning to calm after that scare."

He laughed wryly. "So's mine. It was a frightening thing. Don't ever go near the river again without me."

"Believe me, I won't."

"Good, because you came seriously close to losing your life. No jest."

"I know. I've never felt so helpless in my life. I hate that feeling."

"Why did you never learn to swim? You've spent plenty of summers up here, at least a dozen by now."

"My parents considered it a hoydenish thing to do. Proper young ladies did not jump into the water. They stayed indoors and protected their alabaster complexions. They worked on becoming accomplished. I had lessons to become proficient on the pianoforte."

"You play nicely. I've heard you a time or two."

"Oh, thank you. I'm much less proficient in painting and dancing. I had lessons in those, too. And endless tutorials on how to hold a fan. I learned languages. French. Italian. Because one never knew when an Italian prince or French comte might walk into one's life. But nothing could be better than an English peer. I was forced to memorize Debrett's list of peers and peerages."

"I'm sorry. I had no idea your family squashed the life out of you."

"They did. They really did. But you could change that."

He stiffened. "How?"

"For pity's sake, you can start breathing again. It is nothing dreadful." Well, he might think it was an awful idea. Although, why would he? She wasn't asking him to seduce her or…heaven forbid…marry her. "Do you…would you…that is, I ought to learn how, don't you think? Because if I am chased, as I surely will be once Father's men catch up to me, it would be convenient not to drown."

"Blessed saints! Are you asking me to teach you to swim?"

"Yes. What did you think I was asking? How else am I to help myself?" He had called her a squashed thing. Her betrothed must have also considered her to be this same nothing of a girl, one he could cheat on and laugh at when he was caught. "I could pay you for the lessons."

"Don't insult me, Katie. I'm not taking your money."

"I'm sorry. I wasn't trying to be rude." She hadn't seen him since her fifteenth birthday. After that debacle when he'd landed drunk atop her – and obviously did not remember it – he'd returned to university and she'd gone down to London with her parents. She knew he was often in London and that he belonged to the infamous Wicked Earls' Club.

She thought about him on those rare occasions when she passed by Bedford Place where the club was quartered. All sorts of wicked goings on occurred there, she'd been warned. Not that she would ever consider entering such an establishment.

Perish the thought!

She'd also noticed him at the various balls and other entertainments held throughout the season, but he usually traveled with a fast crowd and never paid her any notice.

"You haven't changed much, Niall." He was still exceptionally handsome as he'd matured into a man. The firm cut of his jaw, his perfectly aquiline nose, broad mouth, and eyes that always held a gleam of mischief. They were still the vivid blue of a May sky, almost ensorcelling in their depth and brilliance.

His hair color hadn't changed much either. He still had a head of rich, golden hair that looked stunning on him when wet and slicked back, but also looked just as good as it dried under the heat of the sun.

He laughed softly. "And you've changed completely. I mean that as a compliment, Katie. You've filled out nicely. I expect you'll look quite pretty once you dry off."

"Did you not think I was pretty before?" His remark hurt her feelings, not that he ever had a care what he said or how he hurt her. He wasn't mean, really. He was just careless, and would usually apologize once he realized it.

He was quite sincere about his remorse, too.

So, despite never wanting to like him, she sometimes did.

She also liked the way he stood up to people who tried to foist rules on him.

At those times, she would quietly cheer him on.

But he never bothered to look at her.

"Of course, you were pretty. But you were a child. There was a five year difference in our ages. I was not going to consider you as anything more." He placed a big, warm hand against her waist to secure her in the saddle. "What I thought back then doesn't matter. We both know I was a complete and utter idiot and a wastrel."

She laughed. "Yes, that's true. You were, at times."

He was never really an idiot, but he certainly had been a wastrel. Yet, he'd always had a good heart. It was something he was often reluctant to show. She assumed his careless habits were his father's bad influence. Or his grandfather's.

These elder Jamesons were known to be straying hounds.

But Niall was different.

She knew it and felt it to the depth of her soul.

Because if he was like them, then he would have already found himself an heiress to marry. He would not have had to dirty his own hands with the heavy toil of fixing up his estate. After securing his bride's fortune, he could have returned to his sordid London clubs and spent his days in idle pastimes and his nights in debauchery.

But he hadn't done any of it.

Well, he was a bit of a womanizer.

That would end when he fell in love and married. Again, she felt it in her soul. He was a decent, honorable man. This is who he really was.

She did not understand how or why she'd come to this conclusion. Perhaps it was because he had the hands of a laborer, rough and callused.

Was it wanton of her to like the way they felt on her body?

Oh, good heavens.

No!

They rode the rest of the way to Alnwick Hall in silence.

As they drew nearer, she noticed improvements to the manor and grounds. "Niall, you've done a fine job. The hall is looking better than I've seen it in years."

She turned slightly to glance at him, and found him looking at his home with pride. "My father and grandfather never did much to keep it up. I'm trying now, but it's slow going."

"You'll get it done. I know you will. I'll help you while I'm here."

He laughed, his breath soft against her ear. "You'll ruin your delicate hands."

She shrugged. "I'm not made of porcelain. I can be useful. What would I do otherwise?"

"Don't you have more on your mind than to think of fixing your wastrel neighbor's mess?" But he seemed pleased by the offer. "You need to consider what you're going to do about Yardsley. A bridegroom's infidelity is not necessarily sufficient grounds to end a betrothal. Is there a chance he is willing to let you go?"

"A very good chance. I'm sure of it. He never liked me all that much. I don't even know why he chose me out of all those young hopefuls. Perhaps because his family was leaning on him to marry. He thought I was a timid drudge who would put up with his womanizing and other arrogant foibles without complaint."

"Then he's a great fool," he said with surprising anger.

"No, I was the fool for going along with it. I was nothing more than a wealthy door mat for him."

They'd now arrived at Alnwick Hall.

He dismounted and placed his hands around her waist to help her down. But to her surprise, he did not immediately release her.

Not that she cared.

If he wished to hold her, she was not about to gripe about it.

"Can you stand on your own?" He was looking at her as though seeing her for the first time.

"I'm sure I can."

"Because I thought your legs might buckle. You look spent, as anyone would if they'd taken the mail coach from London to here. You probably got very little sleep. Then you walked all the way from St. Michael's Priory. Not to mention the dip you took in the river a little while ago. Perhaps I had better carry you inside."

"Oh, that's actually thoughtful of you." She cast him a hesitant smile.

He chuckled. "It is, isn't it? Good grief, Katie. Too long in your company and I might turn into a bloody saint."

"I'm sure there's little chance of that." She put her arms around his neck as he took her back in his arms and carried her into his big, rambling house.

A shocking thought struck her the moment they passed through the doorway.

They'd crossed the threshold!

As in…I'm carrying my bride over the threshold to signify our new life together as husband and wife.

Yardsley, the toad – yes, she thought of him as a lowly toad she'd love to squash beneath her boot – would never have done this.

But Niall had.

Did it signify anything?

CHAPTER THREE

NIALL WAS NOT going to think twice about what he'd just done, carrying the Perfect Miss Pringle into his house as though she was now to be mistress of his home. His sanctuary. Well, she wasn't.

She would never be his wife.

He was not going to marry a paragon of perfection and spend the rest of his life walking on eggshells to please her.

But he would carry her upstairs to Phillipa's room since there were no other guest chambers properly aired out and readied for company. "My cousin won't mind if you use her bedchamber. She won't be back for another week, so you would not be putting her out."

"How is Phillipa? I look forward to seeing her."

"She's at a house party at Lord Wrexham's country manor. He's taken quite a fancy to her and she rather likes him, too."

"A love match?" She sighed. "I'm so happy for her. I've always liked your cousin. She deserves the best."

"And she's always liked you." He opened the door to Phillipa's bedchamber and carried Katie inside. "Take whatever you need."

He set her down and forced himself to take his hands off her, not quite understanding why it was so hard to do. "I'll send Mrs. Crisp up to assist you. Her husband and I will bring up a tub and hot water for your bath."

"It seems an awful lot of bother. I can wash my hair in the basin." She pointed to the ewer and basin atop the bureau. "As for the rest of me, I can scrub myself down with the remaining water. All I need is a washcloth and soap."

"It's all right, Katie. We don't mind spoiling you a little today."

She started to thank him, but sneezed instead. "Oh, dear."

"Here, let me help you with the laces. You had better get out of that wet gown right away." Heat shot through his entire body the moment he came up behind her and loosened those wet ties. *Bollocks*. He'd barely touched her.

But they stood achingly close.

And her body – good heavens – those full, pert breasts and long, slender legs would turn any man into a mindless, rutting ram.

He turned away as soon as he was finished and flung open the doors to his cousin's wardrobe. He found nothing but light, summer clothes in there. Not even one serviceable woolen wrap. He removed the only robe he could find, a thin, silky thing. "Here, put this on until the bath is ready."

He strode out before he did the unthinkable and kissed her. The mere notion of Katie's soft body hidden under nothing but silk had turned him to fire.

Obviously, he was delusional.

Him and Katie Pringle?

The idea was laughable.

He strode downstairs in search of Mrs. Crisp, knowing he only needed to follow the heavenly aroma of lamb stew into the kitchen to find her.

He saw her bending over a large pot, stirring the stock for the stew. "May I have a word, Mrs. Crisp?"

"Yes, m'lord. I assume it has to do with Miss Pringle? I saw you carry her upstairs."

"It's all innocent. You don't need to hit me with your spoon and tell me what a good girl she is and what a despicable knave I am." He quickly explained all that had happened to Katie.

"Blessed day! And you've left the lovely lass alone to fend for her herself after all she's just been through? She must be shivering. Here, take up this pot of tea and a slice of last night's apple tart. This ought to hold her for now. I'll find Mr. Crisp and have him help you bring up the bath and water."

Niall stared at the tray she'd just shoved in his hands.

"Well, go on with you. Don't keep the sweet girl waiting." She tried to shoo him out of her kitchen as though he were nothing more than a cat underfoot.

But he stood his ground and attempted to shove the tray back at her. He was a bloody earl, not a hired maid for the girl. "You ought to be the one to bring it up to her."

"I need to find my husband and finish cooking. Why are you suddenly so reluctant? Are you scared of Miss Katie?"

He snorted. "Why should I be? Of the Perfect Miss Pringle?"

Mrs. Crisp frowned. "That is not a nice thing to call her. You'll hurt her feelings. She's always been kind toward you. It isn't fair of you to mock her, especially now that she's had her gentle heart broken by that wretched lord."

"Fine. Stop boxing my ears." He carried the tray upstairs and knocked lightly at her door, knowing his housekeeper was right. Yardsley had treated her abominably and it would be shameful of him to behave as boorishly.

The door flew open and Katie greeted him with a big smile on her face. "Mrs. Crisp, how lovely to–" Her eyes widened and a fiery heat shot into her cheeks, turning them a pretty shade of pink. She gathered the robe about her, Phillipa's silk robe that was obviously too big for Katie, which explained why it was partially slipping off her shoulders.

He almost spilled the tea on himself.

She ought to have looked ridiculous in it, but she looked like a seductive, kittenish bundle. Indeed, she looked remarkably splendid in the pink silk that did not so much hang upon her body as deliciously hug it.

He took particular note of how the silk fell worshipfully over her soft, round breasts.

Bloody nuisance that.

He glanced at the bed, then silently chided himself for the slip. His body was eager to cavort there with her, but his brain – as boiled and useless as it often was – thought better of it.

However, the little fool had placed her unmentionables over the footboard, in his plain sight. Which suggested she was completely naked beneath the robe she was still clutching in her soft and slender hands. Not merely suggested this fact, but screamed it at him…naked Katie…take advantage…slip it off her.

The thought should have revolted him.

Sadly, it did not.

His heart, as well as that treacherous lower part of him, was going to burst if he did not get his mind off her. It did not help that she seemed to be having trouble holding this vapor-thin garment together. "Katie, move aside and let me set down the tray."

The robe slipped open a bit farther. "Oh, of course. You startled me. I expected Mrs. Crisp."

"I know," he said, trying to sound calm as fireworks exploded behind his eyeballs and threatened to erupt lower. "She commanded me to bring this up for you while she finished preparing our meal. I may be the Earl of Alnwick, but she's firmly in charge. I answer to her, not the other way around."

Katie emitted a trill of laughter. "I knew I adored the woman for a reason."

"Well, it seems she adores you, too." He grinned as he turned away to set the tray down on a small side table by the window.

He purposely kept his back to her, afraid to look at her. He was a Wicked Earl, even had a stick pin in the shape of a 'W' to denote his membership in the elite club. But he would never fall so low as to take advantage of Katie.

"Thank you for bringing me the pot of tea. It is just the thing. I am a bit chilled."

"I know…I mean, I expected so." He'd noticed the proof of it while gawking at her breasts. Lord, he'd fallen so low.

"Niall, I think we have a problem."

He busied himself pouring a cup of tea for her because he was still too cowardly to face her. "What sort of problem?"

"Phillipa's clothes won't fit me. She's taller than I am and built quite differently. I'd have to alter her gowns and it wouldn't be right. I'd ruin them for her." She came around to face him and took the offered cup from his hand. "Does she have any clothes from her younger days?"

"I don't think so. She didn't visit much when she was younger and her parents were alive." He'd been appointed Phillipa's guardian even though he was only a few years older. Her father had named him in his testament and some idiot judge had upheld it.

Him?

A trustworthy guardian?

Well, he'd done his best to look out for his cousin.

"What shall I do? I don't have anything else to wear and I cannot order my own gowns brought over from next door or my father's staff will know I'm here. Their loyalty is to my father, not me."

He raked a hand through his hair as he gave the matter consideration.

The only idea he could come up with in the moment was not very clever. Indeed, it was almost absurd. "I'll give you some of my childhood clothes. Phillipa keeps nothing here other than the gowns and accessories in this wardrobe. Would you mind wearing a pair of boy's breeches?"

She gasped and cast him an endearing smile. "I would love that! I was always made to dress in bows and lace and forced to wear delicate slippers that were good for nothing but sitting politely. I couldn't run in them. Or go outdoors without getting them soaked. All I ever wanted to do was toss them aside and climb the apple trees in our orchard."

"You did?" He was genuinely surprised. She'd always seemed so smugly content, sitting quietly and looking like a doll on display in her starched, white gown, matching white gloves, big white bow in her dark hair, and strand of pearls glistening at her throat. "Well, that is something we will have to attend to before you leave Alnwick."

He had no idea she'd been feeling so confined and unhappy.

Her eyes were as big as emerald moons. "Seriously? You would do this for me?"

"It will be my pleasure." All the adults had frowned at him and called him a heathen while he ran around wildly, scraping his knee, tearing his breeches, and always dirtying his clothes. Meanwhile, poor Katie had been tortured by watching him have fun and never being able to participate.

He was going to remedy this. "I'll give you one of my caps to hide your hair when I take you to the orchard tomorrow. We'll steal your father's apples and bring them home for Mrs. Crisp to bake in a pie."

Her eyes could not contain their sparkle. In truth, the entire room seemed to suddenly shimmer with their light. "Hurrah! That sounds perfectly wicked. I've never stolen anything before in my life."

He caressed her cheek, quite charmed by her enthusiasm. "Katie, you are a Pringle. These are your apples. I'd be stealing them. You wouldn't be."

He laughed at the look of disappointment washing over her face. "But I'm sure your parents would be horrified to learn that you were dressed as a boy and climbing trees. Not to mention abetting me while I stole your apples."

He cupped her pert chin in his hand and gave it a gentle tweak.

The beautiful smile returned to her face. "Well, that's all right then."

He cleared his throat and released her before he did the unthinkable and kissed her. "I'll be back shortly with your tub. Drink your tea. You need to warm up."

And he needed to be iced down.

He returned downstairs to the kitchen, intending to lean over the sink and pump cold water over his head, but Mrs. Crisp and her husband were already waiting for him. He and Mr. Crisp carried the tub upstairs instead.

His heart began to pump harder now that he was back at her door. She'd left it ajar. "Katie, make yourself presentable. We're here with the tub."

She pattered to the door in her bare feet and held it wide for them. He was relieved to see that she'd done a better job of wrapping the robe around herself, although she still looked irresistibly delicious. "How lovely to see you again, Mr. Crisp. How have you been?"

"Can't complain, dearie. But you've certainly set London on its ear."

She blushed. "It is rather a mess."

"Never you worry. It'll all work out. You're safe here for as long as you wish." They set the tub beside the hearth. "His lordship will never tattle. Nor will the missus and I."

"I appreciate your kindness more than words can say."

"We'll be back in a trice with the bath water," Mr. Crisp assured, striding back out.

Niall lagged behind a moment. "I'll help Mr. Crisp bring up the buckets then search the old trunks for my boyhood clothes."

He turned away and strode out the door before she could reply.

But it was little reprieve, for he was in and out of her bedchamber another three times, carting in buckets of water that were as steaming hot as the blood coursing through his veins. Once the chore was completed, he marched to his own chamber and stripped out of his clothes. Since he'd already washed in the river, he merely changed out of the dirty work clothes and put on clean ones.

He did not bother dressing like a gentleman.

It seemed a waste of time since Katie was going to be sitting beside him in breeches anyway. Once changed, he ran upstairs to the nursery and began to rummage through the old trunks. All his boyhood clothes were in there. Well, at least the ones he hadn't managed to destroy.

He grinned, imagining what Katie would look like in them.

He drew out several shirts, knickers, vests, and jackets. Then he grabbed some socks and boots, and finally, two caps. Feeling quite proud of himself, he strode down to her bedchamber and knocked lightly at her door. "Katie, it's me. Are you decent?"

"No! I'm in the tub." He heard the soft splash of water as she obviously panicked and tried to sink down low enough to cover her body should he ignore her warning and march in.

A man's brain was a shameless thing. Instantly, it sank low as well. He wasn't purposely trying to thinking of her naked.

Nor would he open that door.

But how was he to hand her the clothes?

Mrs. Crisp angrily poked her head out a crack and grabbed the clothes out of his hands. By the fierceness of her scowl, she was obviously aware of the depraved workings of his mind. "Do not dare come in here," she warned before shutting the door in his face.

"I wasn't going to ravage the girl." Outright lie and Mrs. Crisp knew it.

"Fat lot of thanks I get for trying to be helpful."

He heard Katie giggle. "Thank you, Alnwick. I appreciate your thoughtfulness. Now go away. I'll join you for supper shortly."

"And do not disturb us again," Mrs. Crisp added with a grumble.

The harridan was not going to guard the girl day and night was she?

Besides, why should he care?

These stirrings of desire he was suddenly having for Katie were merely an aberration. He'd return to his senses in a moment. Indeed, he was already not thinking about Katie soaping her body or how beautiful she would look with water glistening off her breasts.

He made his way downstairs and went to the stables to check on Templar to make certain the valiant steed was properly curried and fed.

Katie was just coming downstairs to join him in the dining room when he strode back inside about twenty minutes later.

She looked too delicious for words.

He grinned as he held out his arm to escort her to supper. "My clothes fit you."

She laughed and shook her head. "I'm still getting used to them, but I love how they feel on me. Quite liberating."

Her hair was damp and had merely been brushed back off her extraordinarily pretty face. Her hair was longer than he'd realized and those dark curls were spilling down past her hips, covering much of her shapely bottom.

He tried to ignore the effect she was having on him.

Why should she be special? He'd bedded plenty of young ladies with long, dark hair, and even some with emerald eyes.

But Katie's eyes held starlight.

He'd also kissed many a young lady's soft, pink lips…and soft, pink breasts, if he wanted to be crude about it. He shook out of that low thought, because he was never going to kiss this girl's breasts.

He wasn't going to kiss her anywhere on her body, not even innocently on her lips.

His body was a roiling mess by the time he led her to her seat at the table. Mrs. Crisp had placed her beside him, obviously deciding to keep them close. Of course, it made sense. They weren't going to shout at each other from opposite sides of the long table. Besides, he would never see her over the enormous, silver epergne sitting decoratively in the center.

But seated so close to her felt uncomfortably intimate.

Why did she have to be so pretty?

Her scent was nice, too. Like orange blossoms. And now his clothes would carry her scent. Well, he hadn't fit into those boyhood garments in ages. They'd go back in the trunk once she was done with them.

He said nothing as Mrs. Crisp served them their stew and placed a loaf of freshly baked bread beside their plates. Mr. Crisp poured him an ale and her a glass of cider. Then the couple disappeared into the kitchen, leaving him alone with Katie.

She closed her eyes and inhaled deeply. "I am going to gobble this meal down."

He smiled at her. "Go ahead. Slop it up with the bread, too. That's what it's there for. I'm sorry it isn't fancy, but—"

"It's perfect." She inhaled again and this time turned glittering eyes on him. "Do you wish to know a secret?"

He arched an eyebrow, wondering what possible secret this innocent girl could have. She had never misbehaved in her life, never even stolen so much as an apple off a tree. "Yes, aching to know."

"This is how I always dreamed my life to be."

He shifted uncomfortably. "What do you mean?"

"Quiet. Pleasant. Nothing fancy. Just like now. A perfect meal and good company. I've always been an embarrassment to my parents. They've worked so hard to make me elegant, a Diamond of the *ton*. But I'm not. I never will be. I was born with an inelegant soul. Well, I don't mean inelegant, exactly. Perhaps humble soul is a better description. I dislike ostentation. I'd be happiest leading a simple, country life."

"That is a dire secret, indeed." He cast her a teasing smile. "But you are wrong about yourself, Katie. You are an incomparable diamond. You are not cut like all the others. Nor do you have their same polish. But that is not a failing, that is your strength."

"What do you mean?"

"Your parents are wrong to mold you like all the other young ladies out in society. Most of them are vapid and dull. But you...well, you are radiant. You...are unique."

"Is that your polite way of saying I am odd?"

"Not at all. You are like no one else. You are cut like no other gem and your shine has hidden depths. You are no mere bauble with outward polish. Your sparkle comes from within. It is intricate and magical."

She said nothing, but he knew she was affected. The little apple in her throat bobbed. "Did you just give me a compliment?"

"Yes." He leaned closer. "Any man with a sensible brain will appreciate your worth. Forget about Yardsley. He's an arrogant boor. And you're right. He won't want you once he realizes you'll stand up to him.

But let's have this conversation later. You must be starved. Eat up while the stew's still hot."

Nodding, she dipped her fork into her plate and began to poke at her food.

"I'm sorry it isn't finer fare," he said, watching her out of the corner of his eye. "But I'm alone here and usually tired after a hard day's work. This sort of meal suits me better than–"

"Oh, I quite agree. Nothing to apologize for," she said, hastily swallowing the dainty dollop she'd stuck into her mouth. "This is perfect. I can't tell you how deadly dull I find all those sophisticated dinner parties and the endless courses we must sit through. I'm often seated at the low end of the table because of my lack of rank. You have no idea how boorish some of my dinner partners have been."

"Even if the host and hostess seated you beside dukes and earls, you'd likely find the conversation stifling." He swallowed a mouthful, vowing to increase Mrs. Crisp's wages once he had two shillings to rub together. The stew was delicious. "The titled despise successful commoners like your father, believing him unworthy of his wealth. Yet, they covet it and will hold their noses to marry into it."

"Or pile it onto their own wealth as Yardsley meant to do." She set down her fork and studied him. "Why have you never married? Don't you wish to find yourself an heiress?"

"I suppose. I've never made a secret of my intention to marry into a fortune. It would certainly make life easier for me." He shrugged. "I don't know. I just haven't gotten around to making the commitment yet."

"I suppose you've been having too much fun as a bachelor." She stared into her plate. "How much of a commitment does it need to be?"

"None, I suppose. Other than an agreement to be discreet in my extramarital pursuits. My father and grandfather before him couldn't even manage that. I expect they hurt their wives. I know my father's antics hurt my mother." He frowned. "Katie, eat up. Is something wrong with your food? Because mine is delicious."

"No, but I just realized…" She cast him a thoughtful look. "The men my father sent to look for me will probably catch up to me in a couple of days. I'm sure he's offered an obscenely large reward for my safe return."

"Yes, it is likely." He took a sip of his ale while waiting for her to explain.

She dabbed her lips with her table linen and cleared her throat. "What if you were the one to return me safely to London? Then the reward would be yours. It would go a long way toward putting your estate in order, wouldn't it?"

His frown deepened. "It would, depending on how large it is. But I'm not going to deliver you back to your family if they're going to insist on your marrying Yardsley. I've told you, you deserve better than that oaf."

She appeared surprised. "Why do you care what happens to me after you collect your reward? I thought you didn't like me."

"I thought I didn't, either," he grumbled. "But not liking you is not the same as despising you enough to participate in ruining your life."

She chuckled. "That is quite noble of you."

He set his elbows on the table and stared at her. "We both know it isn't."

"Well, give my proposal some consideration. I'm not likely to escape whatever fate my parents have in mind for me. It would all seem pointless and wasteful if nothing good came out of it. I mean it, Niall. Don't be so quick to dismiss me. Alnwick Hall is a beautiful house and deserves to be restored to its former glory."

"Yes, it does." He nodded. "But not on the back of your misery."

"I've just told you, I'm going to be miserable no matter what is decided for me. However, why should something good not come out of it? My fate would be more bearable if I knew your home, your tenant farms, and the other Alnwick holdings were given the chance to flourish because of me. Think of it this way, you'd be doing me the favor."

"Katie, no."

She looked like a wounded bird. "So you will allow my entire life to be a waste?"

"You are awfully young to be giving up on your future. No matter what happens, your life is not going to be a waste."

"It is, Niall. There's no need to be polite about it." She bowed her head, no doubt trying to hold back tears.

Bloody nuisance. How could she think he'd ever enrich himself on her unhappiness?

"Just consider it. Promise me you will. After all, someone will eventually find me and take me back to London. Why shouldn't it be you?"

"What if your father insists on your marrying Yardsley? And who's to say Yardsley will refuse? I could be wrong about him. He may decide he likes you with a little fire in your belly."

"No, I assure you. He wants a mouse for a wife. Give it some consideration. I am willing to help you. There is no need for both of us to be denied our happiness."

"Fine. I will consider it." But he wouldn't really. He supposed he was the worst fortune hunter ever to exist. Who ever heard of a fortune hunter with a conscience?

But he could not take money for delivering Katie into an unhappy marriage. Even if Yardsley begged out, who would her father seek out next?

Never him.

The Pringles detested him, mostly because his father and grandfather had been rude to them and always behaved like flaming arses, especially around her father. They considered him to be a lowly tradesmen. Therefore, he was to treated as unworthy of their notice.

No matter how hard the Pringle family had tried to be good, welcoming neighbors, the Jameson men had ridiculed and rebuffed them.

Instead of giving up and moving away, Katie's father had doubled the family efforts to be accepted. In doing so, he and his wife had tied poor Katie in knots, making her live up to an impossible standard because his idiot forebears would never accept her as one of their own.

Fortunately, the local gentry were better behaved than the Jameson earls. They adored Katie and treated her with the respect due a proper young lady.

At least there was that.

He must have hurt her so badly, he suddenly realized. His careless behavior had only added to the legacy of Jameson arses.

He'd showed up drunk to her birthday party.

And she still wished to be kind to him?

Not even he liked himself very much at the moment.

CHAPTER FOUR

NIALL LEFT EARLY the following morning to meet his laborers at the Hobson family tenant farm to make repairs to their roof and barn. Daniel Hobson and his sons were his best farmers, and he was thinking of engaging the younger son, Henry, to oversee the other farms on Alnwick land. Although barely above twenty years of age, the lad had a solid maturity about him that had quickly earned him the respect of others.

His calm manner also went over well with the older, more experienced farmers. It was a good fit, because Hobson's elder son was going to take over the farm when his father grew too old to keep it up, and there was not likely to be a place for Henry. Certainly not once he took a wife and started to raise his own family.

Appointing young Hobson as Alnwick's estate manager was an excellent solution for both of them.

He glanced up at the sky, noting the height of the sun.

He was scheduled to spend all day with his workers, but was worried about leaving Katie alone for too long. What if her father's hired men came looking for her? He could have dozens searching for her by now.

He turned to Henry. "Willing to take over for me? I have some business to finish up at the manor house. Do you think you can manage here on your own?"

Henry beamed. "I'll do my best, my lord. I won't let ye down."

"Good. Summon me if you encounter any problems." With that, he rode back to Alnwick.

It was just noon by the time he arrived.

Mr. Crisp hurried out and took Templar's reins. "Miss Katie is in the kitchen with m'wife."

"Thank you," he muttered, wanting to tell him that he did not care where she was or what she was doing, but not even he would have believed himself.

Katie looked up and smiled as he strode in. "Mrs. Crisp is teaching me how to bake bread."

"That's useful." He eyed the loaf cooling on the window sill, taking care to study it and not Katie, because his housekeeper was watching him like a hawk. He wanted to keep his thoughts about the girl to himself.

No one's business.

She looked beautiful.

This did not surprise him.

He hadn't needed more than a glimpse of her in his boyhood clothes to get his heart racing again. Her hair was bound back in a braid, but he supposed it was safer that way, especially with fires going, and boiling pots and steaming kettles all around.

He walked over to the sill. "Is this the loaf you baked, Katie?"

She followed him over and scrunched her nose. "Yes, my first attempt. Take a small bite. I wouldn't want to make you ill if it turns out to be awful."

"I'm sure it is delicious." He pulled off a chunk, but took a cautious bite. His eyes widened in surprise. "This is good. *Mmmm*. Very good, actually. What did you do to it?"

She beamed with pride. "I merely followed Mrs. Crisp's instructions. But I suggested tossing in a few raisins. I remember how much you always liked the raisin pudding we had at our Christmas parties. Is it all right then?"

"More than all right." He ripped off another chunk and ate it.

You'd think he'd just anointed her empress of the realm, she was so obviously pleased.

"Did you sleep well?" he mumbled with his mouth full. "Your eyes are clearer." *As in, they are bright and gorgeous.* "No dark circles under them."

She nodded. "Yes, very well. Phillipa's bed was quite comfortable. Thank you."

"Let's have our midday meal and then I'll take you apple picking. How's that?"

"Sounds perfect." She turned to Mrs. Crisp. "We'll grab enough to make several pies and perhaps enough to make cider. The apples might still be a little tart though. They won't be fully ripe and at their prime for picking for another two or three weeks."

"You just bring them to me and I'll sweeten them, never ye worry," Mrs. Crisp said with a nod of satisfaction. "I'll add a little sugar and cinnamon and they'll taste just grand."

Niall led Katie into the dining room where place settings were already laid out for them. "Have a seat," he said and held out a chair for her when she seemed to look bemused. "What's wrong?"

She settled in the chair. "I was just wondering…where would you eat if I was not here?"

He shrugged and settled in his. "I'd probably still be with my workers, having lunch with them."

"What about for supper?"

He wasn't certain why she cared, but he supposed she had been a bit of a mother hen even when younger, always wondering what he and her brothers were up to, and worrying they might get hurt.

Of course, her brothers often did come home with minor injuries because boys did not play gently. "Mrs. Crisp usually brings a tray up to my bedchamber for me. I'm often exhausted by the end of the day. Then up at dawn the next morning. Of course, we use the dining room when Phillipa is around or when friends pay a call."

She toyed with the stem of her empty glass. "Do many friends visit you here?"

"No, and I don't encourage it. I see enough of them when I'm in London." He watched while she nibbled her lip. She was fretting, although he did not know why. Then the reason struck him like a bucket of bricks falling atop his head.

Katie, this sweet girl he'd ignored and dismissed for most of her life, worried that he was lonely.

Because she'd been so lonely all of her life.

To prove his point, she cast him an endearingly sympathetic smile. "Do you have no friends around here?"

He laughed. "I have more than enough. I don't mind the solitude, you little snoop. Indeed, I savor it. How else am I to get my work done?"

He reached for her hand and gave it a light squeeze, amazed that of all people, Katie should be the one to think of him and worry about his well being. "It does not bother me to eat alone."

This was not merely about his daily routine. This was about all the enjoyment she'd been deprived of while being molded into someone elegant despite her common heritage. She had never had a playmate deemed suitable for her when she was younger.

She could not even play with her brothers because they were always running off with him, leaving her behind to her tedious lessons.

Her eyes filled with trepidation as she continued to ask him questions. "Do you plan to go back to London anytime soon?"

"Perhaps around Christmas. Katie, truly. I am not unhappy being alone here. I've made good progress on restoring the estate, and there's lots to keep me busy, especially with the harvest coming up soon." He leaned back in his chair and studied her. "My turn to ask questions."

She nodded. "I suppose it is only fair."

"Why did you run to Pringle Grange? There must have been easier places to which you could have escaped. Your father has several beautiful estates in England, at least two that I know of near London."

She nodded. "I'm not sure why. Perhaps because this place always felt most like home to me."

"Truly? Why? You only spent summers here."

Her cheeks turned pink. "The truth?"

"Yes, always."

She sighed and continued. "Because of you."

"Me?" This was a revelation.

"I always found you entertaining. Usually because you were making an ass of yourself, but you always made me laugh. Your jests and antics were never cruel, just silly. My brothers liked you, too. They looked forward to seeing you, even though you were always a bad influence on them."

He arched an eyebrow and grinned. "They never complained."

"Why would they?" She cast him a charming smile. "They had fun misbehaving with you, even if you did give my father fits."

Niall winced. "He never liked me."

"Can you blame him? Your father and grandfather always treated him abysmally. And you…well, you were the bane of his existence. But you always raised my spirits. I'd see you riding up and would immediately start laughing. I thought of you as a dust devil. You know, one of those whirlwinds that tear through one's home and leaves a mess in its wake."

She shook her head, looking mirthful for the first time. "You were a good friend to my brothers. Ralph is now married and settled in Boston. Michael travels all the time since he's being groomed to take over the Pringle businesses. He's too busy to marry, or so he tells me, even though he's the eldest. Jordan is in Scotland building Pringle ships, and when he's not doing that, he's at his stud farm breeding the finest race horses. He's also married."

"They might all be coming up here to look for you then. I hope so. You'll be safest returning to London with them."

"No, they won't be coming for me. They weren't in London for my wedding. They cannot have heard yet about my running off. Perhaps

Jordan has by now, but he will not leave his wife because they're expecting their first child any moment. I don't know where in the world Michael is right now. Ralph is off in Boston and happily settled there. He's not going to run home to search for me when I'll likely be found before he ever receives word."

"I see." Niall's responsibility was clear. He owed it to her brothers to protect her. "Perhaps we had better not go apple picking."

She shot to her feet, shooting daggers at him with her gaze. "Why ever not? Don't tell me you are suddenly feeling brotherly protective toward me? I will not allow it. I want my adventure and no one will deprive me of it. I'll go by myself if you will not take me."

He grabbed her hand. "Sit down, Katie. You ought to know me better than that by now. Of course, I'll lead you astray. Never you worry. It is what I do best."

She grumbled her thanks and sat back down as Mrs. Crisp came in to serve their food, a game pie smothered in gravy.

They spoke no more, each too busy devouring the tasty meal. But Niall's thoughts were madly whirling in his brain. Taking the girl to pick apples was not nearly enough. Yes, he would give her that small adventure, but he would also have to be the one to escort her to London.

He couldn't trust anyone else to keep her safe.

"This is delicious, Mrs. Crisp," she said when his housekeeper returned to clear their plates. "Thank you for a wonderful meal."

"You are most welcome, Miss Katie." The woman beamed.

Niall's heart twisted. Why had he thought he disliked this girl? She did not have a haughty bone in her body. "Come on," he said with a wink, "let's go steal some apples."

He took her hand as though it was the most natural thing in the world for him to do. Only once they'd reached the front door did he realize what he'd done.

Blessed saints.

Why did holding onto her feel so right?

Everything about her felt right.

He paused to properly tuck her hair under the cap he used to wear when he was a boy. He hoped this disguise would fool anyone who came looking for her. "Let me inspect you before we head outside."

Big eyes stared back at him.

No one would ever mistake her for a boy. She had the biggest eyes, framed by endlessly long, dark lashes. Her lips were too soft and pretty ever to be mistaken for a man's lips. Her cheeks were as soft as peaches.

He sighed. "Come on, let's go."

He stepped back to allow her to walk out ahead of him, the gentlemanly courtesy ingrained in him. He realized his mistake at once. Katie was supposed to be a boy and he should not be paying this 'lad' any particular deference or respect. In truth, if pressed, he would say this boy was a grandson of the Crisps, deaf and mute.

It was all he could think of to keep strangers from looking too closely or trying to talk to her.

Katie would kill him for that lie.

It couldn't be helped.

Did she have a better idea?

There was another reason she could not be allowed to walk ahead of him. She had an exquisite bottom that wiggled delightfully every time she took a step. She was temptation itself. He was going to crash into trees if he did not stop ogling her and start watching where he was going.

She hurried down the front steps, then turned to face him when he did not immediately follow. "What's wrong? Aren't you coming?"

"Yes." He certainly was, and she could take that response any way she liked. She'd take it innocently, of course. Meanwhile, he was fighting a ridiculously molten desire to carry her back to his bedchamber and run his hands everywhere along her body.

He truly was an arse.

He'd never liked her.

Why couldn't he remember this?

They walked in silence across the meadow and over the stone bridge that spanned the river. It led from his estate to hers, down a long drive to the Pringle family manor. One could not see the Pringle house from the bridge because the orchard covered much of their grounds.

Most of the apples were not ripe yet, but he caught their fragrant scent on the breeze and knew several trees might have fruit ready for picking.

"Here's a good spot to start," he said, drawing her off the road and into the outer edges of the orchard where the trees got the most sun.

He took a moment to scout out the best one, then made a foothold with his hands and hoisted her onto one of the lower branches. "Niall, we did not think to bring a basket or a pouch. How are we going to get the apples back to Alnwick?"

"We don't need anything. You're going to stuff them down the front of your shirt."

She peered down at him through the thick growth of leaves. "You can't be serious!"

"I am." He reached up to tweak her nose. "Where's your sense of adventure? Come on, be quick about it. I think I hear your father's gardeners coming. Grab a dozen and let's go."

She gave a soft squeal and got to work.

He watched, trying not to burst out laughing as she hurriedly stuffed apples down her front, creating a sort of slide for them between her breasts. In truth, he'd brought along a soft pouch that was now neatly folded in his back pocket.

But watching Katie was too rich to pass up. Besides, she wanted to feel naughty, and this was so much better than merely sticking apples in a pouch. Wasn't it?

He certainly thought so.

She looked so earnest as she grabbed each apple and hurriedly crammed it down her shirt front.

"Careful," he said, desperate not to burst out laughing. "Don't rip the buttons."

It was harmless fun. Surprisingly intimate and exhilarating.

Katie wanted to be wicked.

He was merely providing her this innocent pleasure.

"Are you done? Quick, the gardeners are almost upon us." It was an exaggeration. Well, an outright lie, actually. There was no one around. He would never have allowed her to climb this tree and pluck those apples if there was the slightest chance she'd be discovered. "Here, let me help you–"

She slipped off the branch, emitted a soft cry, and tumbled into his arms.

As she fell atop him, he felt the hard lumps that were the apples stuffed down her bosom. But he also felt the softness of her breasts. An inferno of heat ravaged through him as he wrapped his arms around her to hold her steady. "Katie, are you hurt?"

"No," she said with a shaky laugh, scrambling to her feet. "Let's go."

She took off at a run, waddling mostly because those apples were rolling around her shirt and she was trying to clutch them like a woman carrying a babe in her belly.

He easily kept pace beside her, hanging back a little and keeping alert. No gardeners would be chasing them, but he wanted to be sure no strangers sent up from London to track her down were hiding close by either.

"Is anyone following us?" she asked breathlessly, glancing up at him with vibrant eyes.

He'd never seen this girl so alive before.

"Nobody behind us, but keep going until we're safely over the hedgerows in my meadow." He lifted her in his arms and hauled her over that natural fence of bushes as soon as they reached the Alnwick property line.

He thought she'd pause to catch her breath, but she immediately took off to race through the meadow toward the house. "Katie, slow down. We don't need to run any more. You're safe."

"But we're out in the open here." She gestured toward where his sheep were grazing.

"So what? This is my land. And you are the Crisp's grandson, should anyone ask. Just keep the cap on your head, keep your eyes down, and don't say a word if ever we are stopped. You are to say nothing if anyone attempts to question you. Pretend you are mute. But they won't get near you because I won't let them."

"What is my name to be? I must have a boy's name."

"I suppose." They kept walking quickly toward the house. Even with a jacket that fell below her bottom to hide its shapely curve, he could still tell she was a girl. She moved like one. He'd have to teach her how to walk like a proper boy. "How's Bartholomew? Bartholomew Crisp. It has a nice ring to it."

"No. I need something closer to my name so I'll remember to respond to it."

He frowned. "You had better be mute *and* hard of hearing."

"Fine, but I still do not wish to be called Bartholomew."

They were almost at the kitchen door now. "Caleb. You'll be Caleb Crisp. Although I'm sure all this subterfuge won't be necessary. Come on, let's dump the apples on the table. Mrs. Crisp will be eager to get the pies started."

Her cheeks were a bright pink and her eyes sparkled like gemstones as they tore into the house laughing like children.

His heart lurched when she stuck her hand down the front of her shirt and began to pull the apples out one by one to set them in a neat row upon the table. "Need help with that?" he asked with a wicked arch of his eyebrow and an even wickeder grin.

Mrs. Crisp tried to hit him with her spoon.

Mr. Crisp walked in and saw Katie taking the last apples out. "M'lord, was there something wrong with the pouch I gave you?"

Katie froze with her hand still down her shirt front. "You gave him a pouch?"

EARL OF ALNWICK | 33

Mr. Crisp regarded him helplessly, not wanting to betray him, but not willing to lie to the girl either. Niall took pity on him. "Yes, he did. But you wanted an adventure, did you not?"

She threw one of the apples at him. "You wretch!"

But she was laughing, so he did not think she was very angry.

"Using a pouch would have been the same as gathering purchases on market day. Dull and ordinary. Admit it, Katie. You had fun. You were behaving badly and enjoyed it."

She was still laughing as she removed the last of the apples. "I did. But just to be clear, you are an untrustworthy, utterly disreputable and despicable knave."

"Never denied it." He grabbed one of the apples and took a bite out of it. "Mmmm. It's delicious. Try it." He held it out so she could take a bite and was pleased when she did so without hesitation. Despite calling him untrustworthy, she actually trusted him.

This pleased him beyond measure.

She had to know he would never do anything to hurt her or ever lead her seriously astray. In fact, he suddenly felt quite protective of her.

She scrunched her face and made a sour expression as she munched on the apple.

"I know. They haven't ripened yet. But I like them with a little tartness." Unlike his taste in women. When he took himself a wife, he wanted her soft and sweet. In truth, someone just like Katie was proving to be.

To his own surprise, he'd long since tired of the meaningless relations one could easily find at the Wicked Earls' Club.

The casual decadence gave him very little pleasure now. He wasn't sure why, for his father and grandfather before him had never tired of these one night affairs. Of course, they'd never taken much pride in the Alnwick holdings and hardly gave this estate any consideration other than what they could take out of it.

But he'd always loved this place and now felt great pride in restoring it to the treasure it was meant to be.

He shrugged out of his musings, distracted by Katie's beauty as she removed her cap and allowed her long, dark braid to spill down her back.

Blessed saints.

This girl.

He regarded her thoughtfully.

His father had treated hers as though he was slime beneath his boots. He'd been little better, providing a terrible example for the Pringle sons. If only he hadn't driven her father apoplectic every summer they'd come up here.

The man now hated him.

This would be a problem because Katie – heaven help him – was perfect for him. Indeed, the Perfect Miss Pringle appealed to him as no other woman ever had. He wasn't certain what it was about her. Perhaps it was her wonderment at the littlest things. He enjoyed watching her, was fascinated by her expressions, and could not help being swept up in her excitement.

He had not realized quite how much he'd been missing until their apple picking excursion this afternoon.

When had he ever had such innocent fun? It was all because of Katie.

She'd somehow added laughter to his life.

She made the simplest things enjoyable.

However, he refused to make too much of it.

He may have had more fun this afternoon than he'd had in age, but it was still only one afternoon. She would begin to wear on him the more time they spent together.

They were so different, how could she not?

But what if she didn't?

CHAPTER FIVE

L ATER THAT EVENING, Niall stood beside his window and stared up
at the moon as it glowed against a celestial canopy of darkest black
velvet. After having feasted on the best apple pie he'd eaten in a long
while, and having spent a delightful evening listening to Katie chatter
about her debut season, he was more confused than ever about the girl.

What was he to do with her?

He could not hide her at Alnwick forever. Neither could he find it in
his heart to deliver her to Yardsley. Nor would he deliver her to her father
if he merely intended to turn her over to that arrogant cur.

"Any ideas what I should do?" he asked, gazing up at the moon and
stars as though they might impart some divine wisdom. "I know I've been
a wretched heel, but Katie hasn't. Help her, even if you won't help me."

He waited for a sign.

Of course, it would never come. The sky was silent, the moon quite full
and beautiful.

Silver moonbeams shone on his garden, illuminating the small fish
pond he'd restored just last month.

Bloody hell.

Also lit by the moon were two shadowy figures skulking across his
flower beds.

His heart began to pound.

Had the investigators hired by Katie's father traced her here already?

He hurried out of his room and silently crept into hers. He wasn't sure
how to wake her without having her scream and give herself away, so he
clamped a hand over her mouth. She woke up terrified and immediately
tried to strike him.

"Katie, it's just me." He pinned her down against the mattress. "I'm not
trying to hurt you. But you have to get out of bed and hide upstairs. Your

father's men are here."

The fight died out of her.

Gone was her sleepy haze, replaced by a look of utter fright.

She eased his hand off her mouth. "Already? Niall, what shall I do? Where shall I go?"

"There's a little niche off the nursery. It isn't easily noticed, and I'm not going to let them search much up there. But first, you have to help me make the bed. It has to look as though no one has slept in it."

She nodded. "I can do that."

She scrambled out from under the sheets and immediately began to fluff the pillows while he drew the sheets taut and straightened out the counterpane. It wasn't hard to do. The girl hardly made a dent in the bedding. She obviously did not toss and turn much when she slept.

They were standing so close now that they'd finished the task, he felt the warmth of her slender body next to his. He tried not to think of anything but getting her hidden, but she was wearing one of his shirts as a makeshift nightgown and it only came down to her knees. Not nearly low enough to hide her shapely legs. It was not one of his boyhood shirts. She must have taken it out of his own bureau. "Where did you get that?"

She looked down at herself. "This? Mrs. Crisp gave it to me since my chemise isn't warm enough and nights here can get quite cool."

His heart was pounding again as he began to gather the borrowed clothes she had worn today. The grandson of Mr. and Mrs. Crisp would not be sleeping in one of the family guest chambers. "We need to hide your wedding clothes."

"Don't call them that. I don't want to think about my wedding." But she scampered around the room to collect those garments while he did the same with his boyhood clothes. The shirt she'd worn today now carried the delicate scent of orange blossoms along with the fragrant hint of the apples they'd picked today.

He gathered the last of her borrowed boots and stockings. "Follow me."

"Wait," she said in an urgent whisper. "My pearls. Oh, here they are."

He watched as she put them on, his thoughts now filling with all sorts of improper ideas, most of them concerning Katie in his bed, wearing only that string of pearls.

He was a wretched man.

Truly.

He lit a candle in the hall to guide their way upstairs. Until today, he hadn't been up to the nursery in years. "Careful. Keep close."

She nodded. "Sticking to you like a barnacle to a ship."

He glanced at her to make certain she was all right.

Katie looked pretty by candlelight, her long, dark hair spilling over her shoulders wild and unbound, and her slender body outlined beneath the white linen of his shirt. It suited her quite nicely.

Very nicely.

Too nicely.

He glanced at her full, firm breasts, couldn't help himself because she was naked beneath his shirt and the candlelight revealed this and more.

"Why are you staring at me?"

"Was I? I hadn't realized." Of course, he had been. "Just worried about what else we might have missed."

They'd now reached the nursery.

He set the candle down atop one of the little desks and then opened a trunk to stuff the clothes he'd taken out of there only a few hours ago back in there.

"What shall I do with these?" she asked, staring down at her own clothes.

"Let's make sure we have everything." He began to count the elegant items. "Gown, chemise, stockings. Garters. Shoes. Gloves. Where's your corset?" He started to head back downstairs, but she stopped him.

"I wasn't wearing one. Don't worry. You have everything."

"No, your hair clasps and ribbons. They must still be on Phillipa's dressing table. Never mind. Let me get you hidden and then I'll tuck them in her drawer." He showed her the hidden niche. "Stay in there and don't make a sound until I come back up for you. Do not come out until I open the door and confirm it is safe. If these are your father's investigators, they'll probably insist on searching up here. So don't be fooled by the sound of my voice. I will get you out once they're gone."

He considered tossing in a blanket for her, but the room seemed warm enough. Besides, he did not intend to let these men turn Alnwick Hall inside out, should they decide to knock at his door and request to search. "Niall, be careful."

He kissed the top of her head. "Stay hidden."

In all likelihood these oafs sought to break in like thieves in the night, quietly search for Katie and abduct her if they found her. He wasn't about to let that happen. However, he did want them to search and not find her.

He went downstairs and woke Mr. Crisp. "M'lord, what's wrong?"

"Prowlers." He quickly told him his suspicions. "I don't know if they're carrying weapons. I assume they are. Bring your rifle on the chance they mean to cause trouble."

"Where's Miss Katie?"

"Safely hidden in the nursery niche. We restored Lady Phillipa's room. It will appear as though no one has been in there."

He heard the tinkle of shattering glass. "Damn it," he muttered, adding the broken panes to his list of repairs. "Pringle's going to pay for that."

He lit a kitchen lamp, grabbed one of the hunting guns so that both he and Mr. Crisp were now armed, then headed to the summer parlor where he'd heard the glass break.

Two men had just climbed in through the window they'd managed to unlatch after breaking the pane. They were whispering to each other to be quiet when Niall raised his lamp. "Give me one reason why I should not shoot you gentlemen where you stand."

His caretaker also pointed his rifle at the intruders.

"Hold there, m'lord," one of them said, raising his arms in surrender. "We mean ye no harm. I'm Charles Digby and this is my young associate, Harlan Standish. We're Bow Street runners here on official business."

"Official business? Of what nature? I cannot imagine any that requires you to break into an earl's home in the middle of the night."

"No, m'lord. I will admit we went about it shamefully." Digby rubbed a hand nervously across the back of his neck. "Ye'd be within yer rights to have us locked up, but we beg ye to show us mercy."

"Why should I do that?"

"We're on a very important assignment, searching for a young lady. We need to find her before she comes to harm. Miss Katharine Pringle. She's yer neighbor's missing daughter. We've been hired by her father to bring her home safely."

He arched an eyebrow, pretending surprise. "And you think she's here?"

"Yes. In the vicinity, m'lord. We believe she planned to hide out at Pringle Grange."

"Then why aren't you searching there?"

"We have," said Digby, "but she never arrived. There ain't much between here and St. Michael's Priory where the mail coach dropped her off two days ago. We've been to the other homes in the area and also made inquiries in the village. No one has seen her."

"And now you've come to Alnwick Hall. You think I'm hiding her here?" Niall laughed. "That's rich. Obviously, you do not know my history with the Pringles. I can assure you, if ever a Pringle came to me for help, I'd turn them away. Miss Pringle would not dare step foot on my property. And by the way, I'm sending the bill for the broken window to her father. Let him know that I will shoot out every one of his fancy windows if he thinks to stiff me."

"He'll pay handsomely, I can assure ye, m'lord. But are ye certain ye have not seen the girl?"

"Do I look like I'm entertaining a woman in my home? But I'll be on the lookout for her now. What is she doing here? Isn't she supposed to be marrying the Marquess of Yardsley in London? Good riddance to bad rubbish, if you ask me."

Digby shrugged. "She must have had wedding jitters, I suppose. We'll be in the area for the next few days, staying at the White Stag Inn. Would ye be so kind as to send word to us if ye find her? The father's quite broken up about her disappearance. He had a word or two to say about ye as well, m'lord. But surely ye can feel a parent's worry for his child. We just want to return her to him before she comes to harm."

"So you risked your lives to break in here? I could have shot you and been fully within my rights. Why risk it? A reward?"

"A handsome one," the younger man said, and received a poke in the ribs from his companion. "Well, he's paid us handsome to find her. That's all."

"Don't lie to me. Pringle's probably got every Bow Street man in London on the job, and a fat bonus for the one who finds her."

Digby nodded. "More of them will be up here soon. We can't be the only ones who've picked up her trail."

Niall sighed. "Put down your weapon Mr. Crisp. I think I must let these gentlemen search Alnwick or we'll be swarmed with these miscreants."

He gestured for the intruders to follow him. "Look where you like, but if you break anything or steal so much as a spoon, I shall shoot you dead."

"Understood, m'lord."

He followed the pair from room to room, as did Mr. Crisp and his trusty rifle. "Is it possible she's run off with another man? Perhaps she met him near St. Michael's and they're now on their way to Scotland to elope."

"It is possible," the younger man said.

He led them upstairs. "As you can see, the rooms are untouched save for mine. I can assure you, Miss Pringle has not stepped foot in my bedchamber. Search there, if you like. She believes I am a depraved oaf...which I am," he said with a smirk. "As I've said before. She will not come anywhere near my home."

Digby completed his search of the bedchambers and nodded. "We'll check the barn and then leave ye in peace, m'lord. Our sincerest apologies. But her father is desperate, so we must leave no stone unturned."

He waited for the Bow Street men to leave, then turned to Mr. Crisp. "I have to get Katie away from here. They'll keep coming back. If not these men, there'll be others."

"Where will you take her, m'lord?"

"Back to London. I must. Otherwise, she'll be chased across England and not necessarily by Bow Street runners. Others will come after her, hoping to claim the father's reward. They might not be so kind to her." He raked a hand through his hair. "I cannot leave her to the wolves. Much as I disapprove of her father's aspirations for her, in truth he is a good man. She is safest brought back to him."

"Aye, m'lord. I agree. The sooner you get her away, the better for her."

"Henry Hobson will be bringing supplies to your wife tomorrow morning. He'll be coming here with a loaded cart. As he unloads the sacks of flour and grain, we'll slip her out. Katie's a little thing and can easily hide under a few burlap sacks. Once we are certain no one is watching, I'll borrow a horse for her from Hobson, and we'll set off."

The man nodded. "It is a decent plan."

"She'll have to stay in disguise as a boy." It was the only way they had a chance of her going unnoticed since every searcher would be looking for a young woman. Also, as a boy, she could share his room wherever they stopped for the evening. He did not dare leave her alone. A room to herself was not a possibility. They'd deal with the repercussions once they reached London.

"I'll have my wife pack a pouch of your boyhood clothes for her."

Niall grinned. "I think she rather likes wearing breeches. Far less confining than her elegant gowns. I had better go up and let her out of the nursery. Mr. Crisp, would you be so kind as to keep watch tonight. I don't trust those men to leave us alone. They'll likely not attempt to break in again, but they're going to keep their eyes on the house. As they said, there's little other than Alnwick between the Pringle home and St. Michael's. They know she has to be close by."

"Never you worry, those men will not get near our Miss Katie."

As his caretaker began to patrol, Niall ran up to the nursery. He opened the door to the hidden niche. Katie hadn't moved from her spot. "It's safe for tonight. Those men are gone."

"I heard them searching the bedchambers."

Niall nodded. "I had to let them do it or they would have been watching this house closely. They might still be, but I've devised a plan to get you away." He quickly told her what he and Mr. Crisp had discussed.

He thought she would offer protest, but she merely nodded. "Yes, it's time for me to go home. But you must promise me…"

"What, Katie?"

"You have to claim the reward. I mentioned it earlier, but now I must insist on it. Do it for me, if not for yourself."

He helped her up. "We'll argue about it on the road to London."

She laughed lightly. "You really are an abject failure as a fortune hunter. I've never met a man less willing to sell his soul for wealth and comfort. You had better be careful or others might realize just how honorable you really are."

"Perish the thought," he said with a roll of his eyes. "I am not honorable in the least. And by the way, you'll be sharing a room with me on our journey."

She gasped. "How can I? It will mean my ruin if word gets out."

"You are already ruined. You've run off on your own. The *ton* will imagine the worst. But stay calm, for we will only be sharing the room, not the bed."

She eyed him warily. "Oh, is that so? I suppose you'll get the bed since you're the earl and I'll get the floor?"

He grinned. "The privilege of rank."

He would not let her sleep on the floor, of course. But she was already beginning to think of him as worthy and redeemable, and he truly wasn't. She needed to keep her guard up around him at all times.

Although he made it a rule never to prey on innocents, she was far too tempting a morsel to resist. And he was never all that good at following rules. "You cannot return to Phillipa's room. They'll be watching for any activity in one of these supposedly empty bedchambers. So, we're going to share a room starting now."

She came to an abrupt halt on the stairs and frowned at him. "Did I say you were honorable? You are a wretched man. Why should I not sleep in my own bed when you have a dozen to spare?"

He took her hand and led her toward the elegant earl's quarters. "I just told you. They are going to watch for signs of you in the house. That Digby is an experienced Bow Street man. He got on your trail easily enough."

"But you managed to distract him."

"Maybe. So we have to take every precaution. He and his companion will expect me to be moving around my bedchamber, but the rest of the family wing must remain dark and empty."

She tried to jerk her hand away.

He held on tighter. "Katie, if I am to get you safely back to London, you're going to have to start trusting me. What difference does it make if we start sharing a room now or tomorrow? We'll never make it out of Alnwick unnoticed if you do not cooperate."

"But what will Mr. and Mrs. Crisp say?"

"Not a word to anyone. Not ever. Besides, they'll see the evidence of my sleeping on the floor."

She regarded him in confusion. "You're going to take the floor?"

He sighed. "Of course. Did you really think I would stick you on a pallet instead of giving you my bed?"

"But what about when we travel? The inns?"

"Same rules apply there. I take the pallet. You take the bed. I was jesting before."

"Niall," she said softly, a broad smile on her face. "You really are a gentleman."

In truth, he had no idea why he was behaving admirably toward her.

"No, I'm not. Don't be fooled by a few kind gestures." He did not like this sudden spurt of nobility one bit. "Wait in the hall."

He doused the candle, set it on his desk, and then crossed to his window to peer into the garden where he'd first spotted the Bow Street men. They were still out there, believing themselves hidden amid the overgrown foliage.

Fools.

Their dark shapes were easily spotted under the moon's glow. "Katie, stay low and don't go near the windows. Those men haven't gone away."

"All right." She stood in the hallway a moment longer, nibbling her lip. "Set up a pallet for me. Let me sleep on the floor tonight. I cannot move about freely anyway. One of us might as well get a good night's sleep. It is more important that you do."

"No, Katie. I won't hear of it."

"I'll take you up on the offer tomorrow night. We'll take turns as we travel. How's that for a compromise?"

"I'll think about it."

"No more argument, Niall. We need to be smart about this. Don't be a prideful arse."

He frowned, but ultimately relented since it served no purpose to remain bickering over this inconsequential matter. He quickly prepared the pallet for her by the hearth, giving her his best pillow and a soft blanket. The day had been warm, and even though the night air was considerably cooler, it did not necessitate a fire to heat his quarters. She would be comfortable enough, he supposed.

He tucked her in, still feeling wretched that he was giving her the floor. But she seemed to take it as another adventure. Her big eyes and broad smile were all he saw peeking out from under the blanket. "Sweet dreams, Niall."

"Good night, Katie. Be ready to leave first thing in the morning."

"I will be," she assured him. "You'll have not a moment's bother from me."

Was she serious?

She had already turned his life upside down, first tumbling into the river and almost drowning, and now he had strangers skulking about the Alnwick grounds just waiting for the opportunity to abduct her.

Right, not a moment's bother.

And he was going to spend the next ten days sharing a bedchamber with her, forced to keep his hands off her sinfully hot, little body as they rode from Alnwick to London avoiding all the Bow Street men on their trail?

Jamesons were renowned wastrels.

How long before she wound up sharing his bed?

CHAPTER SIX

KATIE AWOKE JUST before dawn but dared not make a sound since Niall was not yet stirring. She'd caused him enough problems last night by bringing those two unsavory Bow Street runners to his door. Unfortunately, nature called and she needed to attend to it. He'd be angry, but she could not very well take care of the necessaries in front of him.

What if he awoke?

Emitting a soft sigh, she rose and crept to Phillipa's bedchamber, doing her best to be as quiet and unobtrusive as possible on her way out of Niall's quarters. She checked the hall to make certain these men had not broken in again, and remained ever on alert, careful to stay away from any windows and even making certain to avoid the thinnest rays of sunlight.

She moved like a wraith, unseen. Unheard. Leaving not the slightest shadow.

Entering Phillipa's room, she wasted no time in doing what she had to do.

However, she did not rush back to the earl's quarters.

What harm would there be in washing up? The ewer of fresh water and empty basin were just sitting there on the bureau beckoning her. Next to the ewer was a fresh washcloth and Phillipa's favorite soap. Katie picked it up and inhaled the delightfully refreshing and delicate mix of orange blossoms and exotic oils.

She would have to buy this very soap once they reached London. She'd used it in yesterday's bath and loved it. Adding exotic oils was a brilliant idea. Her skin had never felt as smooth or silken.

She quickly washed her hands and face, then could not resist applying it to her entire body.

Was it too much?

Would Niall think she smelled like an orange rind?

Why should she care what he thought? He'd been quite heroic and wonderful these past two days, but she'd known him for years and had not been particularly impressed by his valor before.

Once done, she meant to return to the earl's quarters, but found herself padding silently down the hall to the stairs leading up to the nursery.

She paused on the first step.

Truly, she ought to return to the earl's quarters.

But she was naked beneath Niall's borrowed shirt that she was using as a nightgown. Naked and smelled like a ripe orange.

She had to get dressed.

Feeling the soft, white lawn of his shirt against her skin was most unsettling.

Besides, it did not fit her well at all. She was not very big, almost lost in his shirt. It would fit him like a second skin, of course, for he was muscled and brawny.

She was very much aware that it belonged to him. In truth, the knowledge that his skin had touched the fabric and his divine, male scent had woven itself into the threads, did odd things to her insides.

Truly, it brought out the strangest sensations, this feeling as though *his* body was wrapped around hers.

She shook off the ridiculous thought and crept up to the nursery.

It took her no time to find the breeches, shirt and jacket, and other items of Niall's boyhood clothing she'd worn yesterday. She knew exactly where they'd been placed last night to hide them from the Bow Street men.

She opened the trunk where the clothes were stored, took out the ones she needed, and also drew out an old sheet that must have been used in his crib. Using the sheet, she fashioned a binding to wrap around her breasts in order to better hide their fullness.

Unfortunately, it required her to rip the sheet apart. But Niall would understand and certainly approve. Once properly bound, she quickly donned his old clothes and boots.

It was early yet, so she decided to pack a travel pouch with more of his clothing since she could not wear the same shirt and breeches the entire journey. Mrs. Crisp had left the travel pouch beside the trunk, obviously intending to take care of the chore herself when she awoke.

The poor woman had plenty to do just getting the kettle on to boil and preparing their breakfast, not to mention whatever other morning tasks awaited her.

Proud of her efficiency, Katie quietly made her way down from the nursery and was about to sneak back into the earl's quarters when she was suddenly grabbed from behind, spun around, and pinned to the wall.

All she saw was golden skin and massive muscles.

The scream she was about to release froze in her throat. "Niall! Oh, thank goodness it's you! You didn't have to scare the wits out of me. I was on my way back to your room."

"You little fool," he said with a low growl that sent tingles through her body. "Why did you leave in the first place?" He released a groaning breath and rested his forehead against hers. "I thought they'd taken you."

Did he actually care about losing her?

"I was merely responding to the call of nature. Then after washing up, I thought it was safe to grab my clothes and dress for the day...your clothes, really. I packed more clothes for our journey, but left the travel pouch in the nursery for now. I'll retrieve it later."

"I'll bring it down when we're ready to leave."

"All right." She cast him a tentative smile. "Um, are you planning on dressing now? You really ought to get dressed. Do you think we might have breakfast before we head out? And I suppose we ought to carry extra food with us in case we get hungry later. Or will we be stopping at coaching inns to dine? We ought to–"

"Are you always this annoyingly talkative in the morning?"

"Yes, I suppose I am. My brothers often complained about it. Also, your body has me unsettled. It's big and hot and much too close."

He grinned but did not move away.

She cleared her throat. "I had better brush my hair and pin it up so it fits under that cap." She glanced at the boy's hat on the ground at her feet. She'd dropped it when he'd scared her just now.

He released her finally and bent to scoop it up. "Don't go off on your own again, no matter the reason. Wake me first."

He handed it back to her, but did not move away.

She took it, all the while staring into his magnificent eyes. "All right. I'm sorry I alarmed you."

Merciful heavens.

The man was utterly splendid.

Heat radiated off his body, smoldering and manly. Or was it her insides turning fiery?

He'd slept in his breeches, but had not bothered to don a shirt. Up close, his bulging muscles appeared huge and hard as granite.

Even his stomach was hard and flat. Lightly rippled, too. Like a washboard.

She wanted to touch him.

Of course, she never would dare.

But she was starting to understand why he was such a successful womanizer. Who could resist him? He was awfully nice looking for a dissolute, wicked earl.

His skin was beautifully tanned, unmarred save for a wicked scar that stretched along one shoulder to the back of his neck. It looked like a burn scar. Healed now, but still noticeable.

Otherwise, his body was exquisite. Perfect and golden. He must have removed his shirt while toiling in the fields...under the sun...which he probably had done. "Are you going to keep me trapped against the wall?"

She wasn't scared, just filled with this unaccustomed desire to touch his body. She'd never felt anything like it with Yardsley, which was convenient since Yardsley considered her a mouse and meant to tuck her away in a mouse hole while he cavorted in London.

"Yes, stay right there," he ordered.

In the next moment, he turned away to walk back into his bedchamber.

"Wait." This was most confusing. Was she being punished? Made to stand in a corner for disobeying him? "Where are you going?"

He paused with his hand on the doorknob. "Into my bedchamber, obviously."

"Yes, but why? And why must I stand out here?"

He entered and shut the door behind him, leaving her alone in the hall with her mouth agape.

Had he gone back to sleep?

No, not even he could be that boorish.

How were they going to get along during their time on the road if he behaved this way? In truth, she did not know how they were going to manage their daily routines. He could not toss her out of their room every morning and leave her to stand like an idiot outside his door waiting for him to wash and dress.

The coaching inns they would stop at would be quite busy. They always were. Someone would notice her standing in the hall. What if that someone recognized her?

They'd figure it out, she supposed.

His door opened suddenly.

"Are you–" She yelped when he merely stuck out a hand and unceremoniously drew her inside. "You needn't grab me as though I were a sack of oats."

"And you do not ever leave my side again without letting me know. Agreed?"

She nodded. "And you might have mentioned that you were keeping me out so that you could wash and dress. I thought you'd gone back to sleep."

His lips twitched upward in a grin.

Oh, he was devastatingly handsome when he smiled.

Simply devastating in every way. She inhaled the scent of sandalwood soap on his skin and noticed that his hair was wet. He must have taken a moment to wash it. Men had that luxury since their hair was short and required little fuss.

Hers was too long, practically requiring a ceremony to properly wash it and brush it out so that it dried with just the right amount of curl and lushness to the long strands. It mattered little what she did with it now since she was going to keep it tightly pinned and hidden under the boy's cap anyway.

She took a deep breath, once again reminded of his arousing scent. Clean. Male. Utterly beguiling. What did he think of hers?

Not that it mattered.

Or ought to matter.

She had a mind of her own and did not need his approval for anything. She liked Phillipa's soap and the silky way it left her skin. She adored that hint of orange blossoms. If he did not like it, that was his problem, not hers.

He ran a comb through his wet hair.

She stifled a sigh.

Truly, he was indecently handsome.

"Here, do whatever you need to do with your hair." He handed her the comb. "Do you need help pinning it up?"

She did not want to admit she might need his assistance. After all, she'd just had an entire conversation in her head about standing on her own and not relying on him. "No, I can manage."

Was that a flicker of disappointment in his eyes?

No, couldn't be.

But he was done with his morning preparations and seemed to have nothing better to do than to watch her drag the comb through her dark strands. She made a bit of a show of it. Perhaps it was naughty on her part, but her hair was one of her finer features, and she liked to show it off.

Her lady's maid used to tell her how beautiful it was and how men would fall at her feet if ever she left it long and loose.

She glimpsed Niall's expression reflected in the mirror.

His gaze was steamy.

"Stop dawdling," he said, his voice raspy. "Hobson will be here soon and we have to sneak you onto his cart."

"Fine. Give me a moment to do it up in a tight braid. I cannot have it merely loosely braided. It's a little more intricate to work and I'm not used to styling it that way. It's trickier than–"

"I'll do it."

"You?"

He arched an eyebrow. "Don't you trust me?"

She snorted. "No."

"Sit still and be quiet." To her surprise, his fingers began to expertly weave their way through her mane, his touch gentle. Intimate. Also quite possessive.

It felt odd.

It felt wonderful.

"Done. Open your eyes, Katie."

She'd closed them while absorbing the wonderment of his touch. She now stared at herself in the mirror, turning her head this way and that to inspect the result. "I'm impressed."

He'd done an excellent job, much better than she would have managed.

Of course, he'd had years of practice with women and obviously acquired talents beyond merely undressing them.

The thought saddened her, she refused to think about why.

Perhaps because she'd hoped this was one thing no woman had ever shared with him.

She was mistaken.

Obviously, she was nothing special to him. "I'll take care of pinning it up."

"No, let me do it." He sounded impatient. "It'll be faster."

"All right." She handed him the hairpins.

Once again, he worked with magnificent expertise. "How is this? Secure enough?" He handed her the cap.

She shook her head and patted it. "Job well done, Niall."

He gave a courtly bow. "I aim to please."

Yes, he was quite efficient at pleasing women.

He placed the cap on her head and tucked it low over her brow. "Keep your gaze down whenever we are around strangers. One look at your eyes and they'll know you are a girl. Your lips are a giveaway as well." He raked a hand through his hair. "I don't know if this is going to work. Even if you keep your face hidden, anyone looking closely will know you're a girl the moment you walk."

She frowned. "How can they tell?"

"By the way your bottom wiggles."

"Doesn't everyone's?"

He emitted a pained chuckle. "Lord, no. Certainly not like yours."

"All right, it seems this requires practice. Give me a moment. How hard can it be to walk like a man?" She tried an arrogant strut.

He grinned. "Is this how you think men walk? Like pompous arses?"

"I'll tone it down a little." She tried again, this time keeping her stride more purposeful. "Now?"

"Much better. Try not to be so…intense."

She took a deep breath and let it out softly, then tried again. Her stride was still purposeful, but slower. More casual.

"Try shuffling a little. Don't forget, you are Caleb Crisp, the mute and slightly deaf grandson of my caretakers. Since I was headed to London anyway, I agreed to escort you back to your parents who live in King's Cross. Give it another go."

She kept her stride slow, dragged her feet a little, and kept her head down. But she looked up at him after a moment, curious as to his response. "How was that?"

He turned away and hurried out the door.

She had to double her steps to keep up with him. "Niall, stop. Why won't you answer me?"

"I hear the wagon."

"Liar. You couldn't possibly have heard it rattling up the drive since your bedchamber overlooks the garden."

She was out of breath by the time they reached the kitchen.

Mrs. Crisp was already poaching eggs for them and had slices of bread browning in butter in a pan. She must have tossed a pinch of cinnamon on the bread, for the aroma was heavenly.

Katie hovered over the pan and inhaled deeply. "That smells divine."

When she eased away and turned back to Niall, he cast her a triumphant smirk. "Look over there."

She followed his gaze toward the open side door. Sure enough, Mr. Hobson's wagon had just pulled up at the servants' entrance. "You cannot possibly have heard it," she griped. "This was just a fortunate coincidence for you."

He frowned at her, his smirk now gone and his expression suddenly fierce. "Do you realize you look at the people you are talking to?"

"Yes, I know. Isn't it the polite thing to do?"

"But it will give you away when we travel."

"That's different. I'll be wary once we're on the road."

He folded his arms across his chest, still frowning. "Talk to Mr. Crisp without looking at him. He's just walked in."

She tried. "Good morning, Mr. Crisp."

"And a lovely good morning to you, Miss Katie. I see you are all set for your adventure."

"Yes, I–" She looked at the kindly caretaker and smiled, then hastily glanced down again.

But it was too late. Niall had noticed. "You won't last an hour on the road," he said, grunting in disgust. "This will never do."

She stared at him in dismay. "I know. I'll do better next time."

"Your eyes are huge and they sparkle. Clearly, they are female eyes. *Beautiful* female eyes. You must never look up. Not ever. Do you understand? Stare at your feet. Do not ever look a man straight in the eyes."

"Got it."

"Obviously not. You are still looking at me."

"But it's you. I wouldn't look at any other man this way. Or any woman, either."

He gave a low growl that shot tingles through her. "Others may be watching you as you talk to me. You are to keep your head down at *all* times. What do you not understand about this?"

"Don't yell at me."

"I am not yelling at you."

"Yes, you are. At the very least you are sounding quite angry."

Mr. Crisp chortled and Mrs. Crisp smothered a chuckle as they hurried out to greet Mr. Hobson, and left them alone in the kitchen for the moment.

Niall took her hands in his. "Katie, I am trying to keep you safe. The slightest slip and you'll be stolen away from me. How do you think that will make me feel?"

"Relieved?"

He growled again, that low, beastly growl that made her blood turn fiery and her skin tingle.

"Sorry. I know you will feel terrible about it. You'll worry for my safety and believe you've let me down. But I know that you will have done nothing wrong. If I am captured, the blame falls squarely on my shoulders."

"That isn't my point. I don't care who is to blame."

"You don't?" She stared straight at him, unable to look away from this stunning man who was obviously eating his guts out to protect her. "Then what is your point?"

If she did not know better, she'd think he was about to kiss her.

Heavens! That would be utterly delightful. Kissed by a Wicked Earl? She was not going to resist.

She closed her eyes and kept her head tipped upward, praying very hard for his mouth to crush down on hers.

But all she felt was his soft breath tickling her lips.

Since he wouldn't take that wee, small smidgeon of a next step closer, she tried to lift up on her tiptoes to meet his lips.

But she couldn't do it, for he'd taken hold of her shoulders and gently held her down.

"Katie," he said in a husky murmur that made fireworks explode throughout her body, "what in blazes are you doing?"

CHAPTER SEVEN

B *LESSED SAINTS!*
  Katie was waiting for him to kiss her, Niall realized as her eyes popped open wide and a hot pink blush shot up her cheeks. "I'm not doing anything. What did you think I was doing?"

Had the girl taken leave of her senses?

More to the point, had he taken leave of his?

Yes, he wanted to kiss her.

Desperately, if he wished to be honest about it.

He had no intention of giving her the slightest encouragement. Not for her sake, but for his. The girl was a rampant attack to his heart. She aroused his senses, turned him mindless. His body was in fits and spasms. He was losing control…and he hadn't even had his breakfast yet.

Those big eyes of hers.

Had they always been this beautiful?

And those soft, heavenly lips that – yes – were made to be kissed by him.

What was wrong with him?

He was not some human pendulum to swing back and forth wildly.

How could he go from not liking this girl to being utterly beguiled and fascinated with her? And why was he suddenly terrified of kissing her?

He was a Wicked Earl. He kissed women all the time. He was quite expert at it. Kissing was among the least wicked things in his repertoire. Harmless, really, if one were kissing the sort of woman he usually kissed.

But Katie was achingly innocent.

If he kissed her, it would be the most wantonly exciting thing she had ever experienced.

This was the problem.

After he kissed her, she'd look up at him with that magical sense of wonderment.

How could any man resist her after that?

The Crisps and young Hobson marched back into the kitchen. The elder Mr. Hobson was also with them.

"Good morning, Henry," he said to the burly young man who was now bringing in supplies from the wagon, carrying in two at a time on his big shoulders as though they weighed no more than feathers.

He nodded in greeting to his father as well. "Thank you for riding over with your son. Those Bow Street men will think twice about stopping the wagon if there's two of you on it. Did you notice anyone hanging about Alnwick Hall on the way over here?"

"Aye, m'lord. Two unsavory characters, just as you warned. We pretended not to notice them, although they were not trying particularly hard to hide themselves away." The elder Hobson cleared his gravelly throat, and then cast a glance at Katie. "The sooner you get Miss Katie away from here, the better."

Henry nodded. "We'll do our best to lead them astray. Da's spread the word among the other tenant farmers to be on the lookout for more strangers."

Mrs. Crisp gave a nod of approval. "Aye, and if we're approached again by those scoundrels, we're going to tell them you headed north to Scotland to elope with Miss Katie. If any more of those knaves come sniffing about, we'll tell them the same thing."

Katie smiled at his housekeeper and the Hobsons. "Thank you. I cannot tell you how much I appreciate the kindness you've all shown me. I apologize heartily for requiring you to lie on my behalf. No matter what happens to me after this, I shall never forget any of you or all you've done to help me."

Niall groaned inwardly.

The Crisps and the Hobsons had beaming smiles on their faces, utterly charmed by the girl. Young Hobson's eyes suddenly turned watery.

Bollocks.

What's this?

"It is the least we can do, Miss Katie. My da and I have never forgotten how kind you were to me the year you and your family remained up here through apple picking season."

His father gave a grunting nod.

Henry, the big, hulking bull of a lad, wiped his eyes before proceeding. "I was but a boy when I fell off a ladder in your orchard. I was pulling the apples off the higher branches, lost my footing, and tumbled. My da carried me to the Grange seeking help to fix my broken arm. You must have heard his shouts, for there you suddenly were."

"A proper little lady," his father interjected.

"Aye, dressed in your elegant lace and silk, taking hold of my hand all the while Pringle Grange's caretaker worked on me."

"Mr. Bevins was a good man," said Mr. Crisp, also feeling the need to interject a comment.

Henry was still teary-eyed. "Then you insisted on having Mrs. Simms pack a basket of food for me and my family since we were now down a worker for the month."

"I remember," Katie said gently. "You were a very brave boy. Never howled or wailed the entire time Mr. Bevins tended to you. I marveled at your fortitude."

"And you insisted on sending over a proper doctor to check on my lad afterward," his father added. "Then you came to visit us. I still remember the sour look on your governess's face. But you had the smile of an angel."

Henry nodded. "We never forgot your generosity. It took courage for a little thing like you to stand up to your elders. You could not have been more than nine or ten years old at the time. Same as me." He grinned inanely. "But you held firm, insisting that you were lady of the house in your mother's absence. I think she and your father had gone to York for a few days. No matter, I suppose. You did them proud. You were a grand, little lady."

Katie laughed. "I assure you, I was nothing more than a stubborn child."

But young Hobson's eyes were still watering. "No, it's as my da said. You were our angel."

Bloody hell.

One would think the girl wore a halo on her head and had sprouted wings.

Now the elder Hobson's eyes were tearing. "My family will never forget you, nor will we ever betray you. No one in these parts ever will. They know what you did for my boy. You're the angel of Pringle Grange. That's how we all think of you."

Niall groaned again.

This girl he'd grown up teasing and tormenting was a bleeding saint.

Obviously, he'd been an unmitigated idiot not to notice the kindness in her heart.

He stayed silent while they all sat around the kitchen table and polished off the delicious breakfast Mrs. Crisp had prepared for them.

Then, it was time to leave.

Katie pursed her lips. "How am I to get into the wagon unnoticed?"

Niall pointed to several sacks filled with table linens. "In one of these. Henry's mother does sewing for many of the grand homes around here. We'll just stick you in one of these empty sacks and young Hobson will hoist you over his shoulder and carry you out with the rest of cloths that need sewing."

"Oh, I see. What about my travel pouch?"

"It'll be up front with us," Henry's father said. "Same for his lordship's pouch."

Niall nodded. "About an hour later, I'll ride off as though merely riding into town. The Hobson farm is along the way. That's where I'll pick you up. Mr. Hobson will have a horse for you. We'll leave from there."

Katie's lips remained pursed. "Isn't it an awful lot of bother? If they suspect I'm with you, they'll just follow you wherever you go."

He shrugged. "It is a risk we'll have to take. But I'll be riding out as though dressed for field labor, and Mrs. Crisp is going to leave her famous pies cooling on the window sill."

Katie laughed. "Brilliant. Those men must be starved by now."

Mrs. Crisp clucked like a mother hen. "I wish I could pack you up some decent meals for your journey. You'll fade away to nothing by the time you reach London."

Niall tossed her a wink. "I'll take care of Miss Pringle. She'll be plump as a Christmas goose by the time we reach town."

Now Mrs. Crisp was crying.

He cast her husband a warning scowl. "Don't you start bawling, too." But he soon relented and grinned at Katie. "They never cried over me. Then again, I'm no angel."

"That's right!" Mrs. Crisp smacked him lightly with her spoon. "Ye had better treat her like a lady. I want your oath that you'll behave like a proper gentleman. None of that bad behavior you and your rascal ancestors are known for."

He arched an eyebrow, not really angry with the woman who'd been more of a mother to him than his own. He'd loved his own mother, of course. But she'd always been a weak and tender thing, hiding away and waiting to die after his father broke her heart. "You do realize you've just struck an earl."

She wasn't in the least remorseful. "I've struck a naughty boy. One who enjoys my cooking too much to ever be rid of me. But I need you to behave like an honorable earl and protect our angel, even from yourself."

"Especially from yourself," Mr. Hobson muttered, casting him a warning glance.

He sighed. "You have my oath. You did not need to ask for it. I know Miss Pringle's worth. Not even I could behave fiendishly toward her."

Katie turned to him in amazement.

He saw the puzzled look in her beautiful eyes. *Is this why you didn't kiss me?* He knew this was the question on her mind.

He turned away and slapped his hands on the table. "Time to get going."

He tried to remain calm and not pace like a caged beast as Katie was loaded onto the wagon and driven in the sack to the Hobson farm.

He remained in the kitchen while Mrs. Crisp baked her pies.

Mr. Crisp settled himself on a crate just outside the kitchen door and whittled something out of wood.

Finally, the hour – which had felt like an entire year – was up. He strode out of the house toward the stable. Mr. Crisp set aside his wood carving, tucked his knife back in its sheath at his hip, and joined him in the stable to saddle Templar for him.

"See you for supper, my lord," he said casually.

Niall nodded in acknowledgment.

He noticed the pair now lurking closer to Alnwick Hall, knowing they'd been taken in by the ruse. However, he also kept alert for newcomers to the area. This would be his greatest concern until they rode further south where he was not as well known.

He stopped at the Hobson farm to pick up Katie, his heart beating faster as she emerged from the barn leading one of their horses by the reins. Her travel pouch had already been fastened to the saddle. He casually studied her, ready to give advice on how to improve her disguise.

However, she did a remarkably capable job. The cap was low on her head and shaded her eyes. Instead of looking up at him, her gaze remained firmly trained at her feet. She walked out with a slow gait, her feet slightly shuffling.

The elder Hobson brought over his own travel pouch while his wife came running out of their home to give him a small sack. "It isn't anything fancy. Just some bread and cheese to hold you over should you get hungry before reaching the first coaching inn."

"Thank you, Mrs. Hobson. It is much appreciated." He turned to her husband. "I'll be leaving Templar and your horse at the Sparrows Inn at Morpeth. Send one of your boys down for them in a couple of days."

"We won't be riding all the way?" Katie asked, sounding quite surprised.

"No. We'll travel faster by private hired coach since we'll only need to stop long enough to change teams and be off again. We may even be able to travel by night along the better maintained roadways once we are further south. There'll be torches lit to mark the way and the moon will be full for the next few days. We ought to take advantage."

She nodded. "Very well. I suppose it makes sense."

"But do not ever let down your guard. You are to stay in disguise even while we are in the coach. There's no trusting any of these drivers or ostlers."

"I understand."

They said their farewells to the Hobsons and rode off at a fast clip. Katie was an excellent horsewoman and easily kept up with him. If riding in a private carriage proved too slow, he could always hire horses for them and simply ride the rest of the way. No need to make decisions about that now.

He'd reconsider once they reached York. They'd be safer once there. It would be easy for them to get lost in the crowd.

But that would be several days from now.

He had to concentrate on making it through these next few hours. The towns they had to pass were smaller and he was well known. Katie's family was also known in the area even though they were usually here only in the summers. One year, as Henry had mentioned, they'd stayed through harvest time. Another year, they'd come up here for the Christmas holidays.

But Pringle Grange was always their summer home.

And a wealthy family in the area was always a thing of note. Even if they had rarely come up here, they would have been known to all for miles around.

Another thought crossed his mind as they rode. "Katie, do you recall the inns where your family always stop on the way up here and back again to London?"

"Yes, of course."

"We'll have to avoid those. You'll be familiar to the staff and we can't risk someone recognizing you."

She nodded. "We always stayed at the finest inns. We should be all right if we keep to the less elegant ones. I'm sure they'll still be comfortable and the meals good, even if they aren't as fancy as those I'm used to."

They rode in silence the rest of the way, stopping only to rest and water their horses. By early afternoon, they were both hungry, so when they paused again to rest their mounts, they also ate the bread and cheese Mrs. Hobson had packed for them.

The day was cooler than usual and the wind gustier. Katie was a little thing and Niall worried that she'd be blown away. But she had no trouble handling the wind or her mare, and they continued to make good time. In cool weather, their horses could travel greater distances without tiring.

Also working in their favor was the condition of the roads. The sun was shining and roads were dry, allowing for better progress than if they had to slog through mud and pouring rain.

"We'll reach Morpeth just before nightfall," he said, deciding to review their plans, especially this first night when traveling together was new to both of them. "Once we arrive at the Sparrows Inn, I want you to wait in the stables with the horses until I can secure a room for us. Make yourself look useful, as though it is your duty to feed and water our horses. You'll attract less attention if you look like you belong there."

She made no protest, so he continued. "I'll come back for you as fast as I can. Do not blush as we're led up to our room. Remember that you are Caleb Crisp, my caretaker's grandson. You are in my charge, and therefore my ward during the journey to London. It will not appear odd that you and I occupy the same chamber, especially since you are mute and partly deaf which means you require extra tending."

"I won't blush. I know what to expect now that I've already seen you naked."

He eyed her curiously. "You mean partially naked. I've only ever removed my shirt in front of you." He frowned. "And that day by the river, I took care not to climb out of the water before you'd closed your eyes."

She cleared her throat.

He burst out laughing. "Why, Miss Pringle! You peeked while I was dressing behind the bushes."

"I...accidentally...well, I was distraught."

"And did not realize I was swimming without clothes? Hah! You knew exactly what you were doing, you naughty thing. Well, what do you think? Did you like what you saw?"

She tipped her head up. "No. I blotted the sight of your thin and pasty body out of my mind."

"First of all, my body is glorious. All the women tell me so. Second of all, you are a terrible liar. Your blush always gives you away." He held up a hand when she opened her mouth to protest. "I fully intend to follow up on this conversation at a later time. For now, let's concentrate on getting you in and out of Morpeth safely. We'll take our meals in our room. I'll stay with you as much as possible, but I also must make arrangements for a hired coach to pick us up first thing in the morning. I'll leave you with a pistol with which to defend yourself if ever I'm not with you. Do you know how to handle one?"

"No."

He raked a hand through his hair. "Well, it isn't difficult. You just point it straight at the assailant's chest and fire."

"But I'll kill him if I aim at his chest."

"You've never shot at anyone before. It is unlikely you will hit him anywhere near his heart. Hopefully, you'll just wing him."

"Hopefully, no one will come into the room when you're not there. Better yet, I'll keep it latched and pretend I don't hear anyone knocking. Don't give me a pistol. If I cannot find it in myself to shoot him, then he will simply wrest the weapon out of my hand, and then I'll have it pointed at me. I will keep a fire iron close by. I won't be so reluctant to hit someone with it since I won't be worried about the blow killing him."

He agreed, mostly because the men who would come for her were likely to be Bow Street runners, not a criminal element. However, depending on the size of the reward her father had offered, there could be all manner of men hunting for her. "That reminds me, I had better pick up a newspaper. Yardsley's runaway bride is likely to be a front page story."

"Assuming they aren't paying the papers to suppress the news."

"They won't be able to bury the story for long. It's too juicy. The entire Bow Street community knows by now you've run away. Especially if there is a reward offered for your safe return, as I am sure there is. The details of that reward will also be headline news."

"A reward which you must claim, Niall."

He frowned.

She frowned back at him. "We've been over this. You have to claim it. This is no small thing you are doing for me. You've left important work undone at Alnwick Hall, not to mention put your life at risk for me. I shall hunt you down and shove the pound notes down your throat if you don't claim them."

"Katie, let's not fight over this now. We don't even know how much of a reward either Yardsley or your father is offering."

She tipped her chin up in the air. "I am my father's precious jewel. He will offer a king's ransom to have me safely back. As for Yardsley, who knows? He never wanted me, but he'll offer a matching reward just to save face. It is pocket change to him."

He packed away the remaining food and rose to collect the horses who'd been left untethered to drink from the nearby stream and munch on the gorse and sweet grass along its bank.

It was well past twilight by the time they rode into Morpeth and down its High Street toward the inn. Most of the shops were already closed or about to close down for the night. The Sparrows Inn appeared quiet, but that was not surprising. Most travelers would have arrived by now and settled in for the evening.

Of course, there would be a few late arrivals, such as he and Katie.

The scent of honeyed ham filtered in the air to his nostrils. The innkeeper and his staff were already busy serving supper to their patrons. Niall glanced at Katie. She was tense in the saddle, already dreading her first test as a boy.

He was tense as well, worried about a criminal element hunting for the girl. Such men could not be relied upon to return her to her father. They could hold her hostage and demand ten times the reward.

He dismounted and pointed to the stable. "Caleb, take the horses to the ostler. Wait there for me."

She kept her eyes on the ground and merely nodded.

The ostler recognized him and walked over to greet him. "Welcome, my lord. I'll take good care of yer horses."

"I know you will, Angus. The boy with me is Caleb Crisp, my caretaker's grandson. He is mute and does not hear well. Be gentle with him. Let him water our horses to keep him occupied. I'll be back for him in a few minutes." He tossed the man a shilling. "Make sure the other boys keep away from him. I don't want him teased or abused."

"I'll box the ears of any lad who tries it!" He strode back to the stable with a warning glower for the young stable hands who were already beginning to gather around Katie. "Get away from his lordship's ward, ye wicked heathens. Anyone touches a hair on the lad and it'll be the whip for ye."

Angus then filled a bucket with water and handed it to Katie. "Here ye go, lad," he shouted in her ear and then patted her on the head. "No one will bother ye."

Niall bit the inside of his cheek to keep from smiling as Katie shuffled away with the obviously heavy bucket in her hand. Water spilled over the lip and dripped onto her boots. He wanted so badly to help her out, but knew it would raise too many questions if he did.

Instead, he strode into the inn, signed for a room, and ordered two meals brought up immediately. "Our horses will be picked up by one of the Hobson boys before the end of the week. I'd like to hire a private coach to take me and the boy to London. Can you arrange that Mr. Gray?"

The inn's proprietor nodded. "Yes, m'lord. When would you like the coach brought around?"

"Shortly after dawn. The days are getting shorter now and we must take advantage of the daylight while we can. I have important meetings in London that I cannot miss."

Mr. Gray glanced toward the stable. "And I'm sure that boy is slowing you down. Forgive me, m'lord. But I heard what you were telling Angus. Never you worry, we'll get you on your way first thing tomorrow."

"I am ever in your debt, Mr. Gray." He strolled back to the stable to fetch Katie, taking her by the elbow and speaking loudly in her face. "Come with me, Caleb. Food. Sleep." He made gestures to convey eating and sleeping.

"You are an arse," she whispered, all the while keeping her eyes down. "Don't overdo it."

He kept hold of her arm as they entered the inn and Mrs. Gray showed them upstairs. "Call upon me if there is anything you need. Your food will be brought up in a few minutes. Do you need a bath brought up?"

"Yes, for me. The boy will make do with soap and a wash cloth. Mrs. Crisp is the only one who's ever bathed the lad. He'll just have to wait until I can deliver him to his parents. But he's capable enough and knows how to tend to himself. He'll manage fine with his own grooming. Nothing special required for him."

"Well, you let us know if you need any help. What a sweet face he has."

Niall's heart shot into his throat. "Yes, a peaches and cream complexion is what Mrs. Crisp says. Unlike my face," he said, scrubbing the bristles of his new growth of beard as he tossed the proprietress a wink. "I'm sure he'll turn into a veritable ape like the rest of us within a few years."

He waited patiently for the woman to show them to their guest quarters. The best rooms were already taken, and although Mr. Gray had offered to remove the occupants from one of these finer rooms, Niall had refused. "Any chamber with two beds, if possible, will do."

The one they were shown was perfect for their needs. It happened to have two small beds. Neither he nor Katie would have to sleep on the floor.

Once Mrs. Gray left them, Niall bolted the door. He then crossed to the window to close the shutters while Katie lit the lamp atop the one bureau in the neatly appointed room. He motioned for her to keep silent.

She obeyed, but pursed her lips in obvious frustration. She began to pantomime her displeasure, gesturing about the bath.

He laughed. "Oh, it isn't only for me. I intend to get you into it first, *Caleb*."

She threw down her cap in outrage. "I am not taking off my clothes in front of you," she said in a frustrated whisper.

Her eyes were big and sparkling, this time with fury. It was probably stupid of him to goad her, but he'd been tense riding beside her all day. Behaving himself with Katie was proving hard to do. Not that he would ever break his vow to Mrs. Crisp. But surely, having a little fun was to be allowed. "I'll have a drink downstairs while you soak. The common room is decent enough. Besides, the innkeeper loves to chatter. I'll find out what he knows about those Bow Street men who approached me at Alnwick Hall."

"They may not be the only ones."

He nodded. "Indeed not. I mean to ask him about anyone else who looks suspicious. Ten minutes is what I'll give you, then I'll come back up and have my soak."

"But it's too dangerous for me to go downstairs while you bathe."

"Who said you had to leave? You're the one who's bashful. I'm not."

She groaned. "You are such an arse."

He tweaked her nose. "I know. But you like me anyway."

She turned away to pick up her cap, which had the unintended effect of showing off her perfectly rounded bottom.

It took her a moment to realize why he was grinning.

She sighed. "Can you not be insufferable even for five minutes?"

He folded his arms over his chest. "Admit it, Katie. You are having fun with me and enjoying this adventure."

"I am not having fun. This is your problem, Niall. You take everything as a lark. Well, I don't. I am scared to death of being discovered and taken from you before I'm safely back home."

He stepped to her side and gave her cheek a light caress. "Of course I know this is serious. But it doesn't mean we have to spend the next ten days living in constant fear. We're taking precautions. And anyone who tries to take you will have to kill me first."

Her eyes widened. "Don't say that! I don't ever want to see you hurt."

"Nor do I, but I'm not afraid of it. Especially not after what you just said."

"What did I just say? Oh, that I don't want to see you hurt?"

He caressed her cheek again. "No, you said that you did not wish to be taken from me. Do you mean it, Katie?"

CHAPTER EIGHT

KATIE WAS SPARED having to respond to Niall's question by a knock at the door. The attentive staff, all of whom recognized Niall and were eager to please him, trekked in with tub, water buckets, and trays of food.

She could tell by the heavenly aroma now wafting through the room that under the lid of the silver tray was a fresh lamb stew and a full basket of hot biscuits.

Her stomach growled.

Niall, being uniquely annoying, patted her on the head and then turned away to toss a flirtatious remark at one of the maids. She was a pretty girl, a few years older than herself, she would guess, and quite buxom.

Katie always thought of herself as moderately well endowed, but this woman's breasts were the size of water buffaloes.

Well, perhaps she was being unkind.

Niall said something stupid about tasting her biscuits, to which the girl replied with a giggle and a suggestive lick of her lips, "Any time, m'lord. They'll always be hot and ready for you."

While he jested with the men and flirted some more with all of the maids, Katie stood quietly in the corner, the cap pulled down over her eyes, and her head bent to stare at the floor. She was all but forgotten amid the fuss everyone was making over him.

When he turned on the charm, he could be quite devastating.

Everyone adored him.

Being Earl of Alnwick alone would have garnered him attention. But to be an earl, and also handsome and charming, had everyone tripping over themselves to please him. But it was also more than that.

She could see the inn's staff truly liked his jovial and engaging manner.

Despite his flirtations, he actually treated the innkeeper and his staff with respect. In turn, they went out of their way to accommodate him in many little ways. With a heftier portion of stew for their meal, a generous tankard of ale for him and cider for her, a scented soap instead of the plain, lye soap, and spare blankets should the night turn chill.

Several of the younger maids tossed inviting glances his way, obviously eager to offer their favors. He was quite adept at warding them off, but she knew it was only because of her presence. The Jameson men were known to enjoy the company of women. This was their weakness.

Could Niall ever be faithful to just one woman?

Not that she cared.

It was merely idle musing.

As soon as the inn's staff had left them to themselves, Niall turned to her. "What's it to be? Eat first or bathe first?"

"I'm starved. May we eat first?"

He raised the lid on the small pot of lamb stew and inhaled. "Excellent suggestion. Dig in, Caleb." He ladled some of the meat onto a plate and handed it to her. "Here, dunk the biscuits in the drippings. Give me your cup. I'll pour you some cider."

"Thank you," she said as he filled it, and then watched as he served himself as well.

They ate in silence, both of them apparently ravenous after their long ride. When they were done, Niall carried the tray of empty plates out of the room and set it in the hall by their door. "One of the maids will take it without having to disturb us. Now, about the bath. I'll head downstairs for a few minutes. Bolt the door behind me."

She nodded. "I'll be quick."

The water did look tempting, but she knew that she could not soak in it to her heart's content as she might have done at home. Still, this was wonderful and she appreciated the chance to wash the dirt off her skin. Her clothes were another matter, but there was nothing to be done about that tonight.

The proprietress had offered to take their garments to be freshened and boots to be polished, but Niall had refused. If they had to make a quick escape, they'd need them close at hand.

Katie sighed as she settled in the tub, but did not dawdle. The soap provided was a sandalwood soap, so she used it to scrub herself down. She did not bother with her hair since it was still firmly pinned up and Niall might be back before she had the chance to finish washing it. Also, she could not leave it wet and unbound on the chance anyone happened to peek in.

She had just finished drying off and wrapping the binding around her breasts when someone rapped at the door. Alarmed, she hastily donned the fresh shirt she intended to use as her nightgown and shoved her legs into her boy's breeches in the event she had to flee.

She was still silently scampering to put on her stockings and boots when the rapping began again. How could she ask who it was when Caleb could not speak?

Just go away.

She put her ear to the door and listened for the sound of footsteps walking away. But no such luck. The person was still there.

It was not Niall or he would have identified himself.

As a precaution, she grabbed one of the fire irons.

The door latch suddenly jiggled.

Dear heaven! Was someone attempting to break into their chamber? She grabbed the cap and stuck it on her head, then hastily donned her jacket. She would climb out the window and hide on the roof if she had to.

Her heart was firmly lodged in her throat when the door bolt slowly began to slide to an unlocked position. A feminine voice called out in a whisper, obviously not realizing Niall had gone downstairs. "Yer lordship, will ye be wanting my company this evening?"

Katie shoved the bolt firmly back into place.

The gall of the woman! What did she think Niall would do with her while a little boy slept in the bed right next to them? Of course, she was that little boy.

Then she heard Niall's deep voice beside their door. "Sally, what are you doing here?"

"I thought ye might like me to service ye this evening."

"No, your services are not required, nor were they requested. Who sent you up here?" He did not sound pleased.

"No one, m'lord. I just thought…seeing as ye're here on yer own."

"I have a boy with me."

"Mr. Gray told us about him. But he's a simple-minded fellow, isn't he? He won't understand what–"

"He is mute, that's all. And a little hard of hearing. But he's a very clever child and will understand everything. Go away, Sally. Do not presume my needs."

The maid muffled a sob and scampered back downstairs.

"Blessed saints," Niall muttered, and then knocked on the door. "Caleb, let me in."

Katie did not blame him so much as simply despise the casual way he'd led his life and how easily the women flocked around him.

He stepped in and quickly bolted the door again. "I suppose you heard that exchange."

She nodded. "Every word."

"I didn't ask for her." He sank onto his bed and began to shrug out of his clothes.

"I know." She set the fire iron back in its mounting by the hearth.

"Then why do you look incensed?"

She turned away. "I'm going to bed. The tub is all yours."

He sighed. "I do not make it a practice to accost the serving maids at the inns wherever I stay."

"Oh, I'm sure they are more than willing to warm your bed. A handsome, bachelor earl? I doubt you ever need to force any woman into cooperating. I'm surprised they haven't broken down our door already, hoping to get at you."

He tossed off his boots and walked to her side, now clad only in his trousers. "Are you jealous?"

She huffed. "Certainly not!"

"Then why are you still casting me that prune-faced scowl? I don't owe you an apology or an explanation, especially since I've done nothing wrong. Even if I had misbehaved, what right do you have to admonish me? I am not your husband."

"Thank goodness for that!" She turned away and folded her arms across her chest.

To her surprise, he came up behind her and wrapped his arms around her. "Do you hate me that much, Katie?"

"No," she admitted because he had behaved like a gentleman toward her, even now as he had his arms around her. It was a loose embrace and she knew that he would release her if she asked it of him. But his arms felt warm and wonderful.

She liked their closeness.

But she eased out of his arms and turned to face him. "It is such a double standard, isn't it? Were I to take a man to my bed outside of marriage, I'd be ruined forever. But a man may do as he pleases and he'll be clapped on the back and admired for his prowess."

"Those are society's rules, not mine. However, there is a logical reason for them. I do not think I'd take a wife who was free with her favors. It is a question of trust. How can I know a child is mine unless I trust the woman I marry? Yes, it is an unfair standard. But it is a matter of necessity. Will some other man's son become Earl of Alnwick?" He snorted. "For all the good it will do him. He'll inherit a heavily burdened estate."

"That was the fault of your father's poor management. But you are doing wonders with Alnwick."

"Thank you. I'm trying my best. It helps that I find myself actually enjoying the hard work." He took her by the shoulders and turned her to face the wall. "Don't peek. I'm about to drop my breeches and take a soak."

She laughed lightly. "Wait. I'll climb into bed and pull the covers over my head." She quickly removed her garments save for her shirt, slipped between the sheets and closed her eyes. "Niall, how was that maid able to maneuver the door bolt? I had it secured, or so I thought."

"Any thin piece of metal can be used to slide through the door at just the right point and move it. I'll prop a chair against the door. We'll hear it topple if anyone attempts to break in during the night. Don't worry about it. I'm a light sleeper. I'll hear the slightest creak of floor boards."

"I hope so."

"Ah, you have such faith in me," he said with unmasked sarcasm, almost sounding disappointed. "Close your eyes. Go to sleep. Sweet dreams, Katie."

"I doubt I shall sleep a wink. Sweet dreams, Niall." She set her head down on the pillow.

The next thing she knew, it was morning and Niall was tickling her nose to wake her. "Oh, bloody murder," she grumbled. "Is it time to get up already?"

He chuckled. "Why Miss Pringle, you have a pirate's foul mouth. The Perfect Miss Pringle is a bear when she wakes up. Who ever suspected?"

"Only when I get up too early." She groaned. "I think I was asleep before my head hit the pillow. And I shall hit you if you insist on remaining as chirpy as a morning sparrow."

He nudged her to a sitting position. "Ah, foul mouthed and violent. This is a revelation."

She opened one eye. "You're dressed. And the tub is gone. When was it rolled out?"

"Last night. You were snoring not so delicately when Mr. Gray and one of his lads came for it. I drew the covers over your head. Horses could have stampeded through our chamber and you wouldn't have heard a single hoofbeat." He cast her an affectionate smile. "You must have been exhausted. But we still have a long way to go. I've had my breakfast."

"Just turn away and I'll change out of my nightshirt. Will I have time to eat a bite?"

"No, Mrs. Gray wrapped up a small basket of muffins for you to have along the way. The hired carriage is waiting for us downstairs. Let's go, Katie. Get dressed. I'd like to be off before others awaken." He leaned closer and inhaled. "Lord, you smell delicious. You don't even smell like a boy."

"But I used the sandalwood soap."

"Yes, but it absorbs differently into your skin. You smell like a blossoming rose petal. Light. Sweet. Irresistible. It's nice. If I allowed myself to be wicked with you, I'd be kissing every inch of your lovely neck."

"Oh." She frowned at him. "Is this what you say to all the women who wake up in your bedchamber?"

"No. Nor do women remain in my bedchamber after we've…done the deed."

"Well, that doesn't sound nice at all. You kick them out once they've…er, satisfied you?"

"It's by mutual agreement. All the more reason I never involve myself with innocents such as yourself." He knelt beside her to assist her in buttoning the falls of her breeches and then crossed to the hearth to fetch her boots. "You'd expect the world if you and I ever did…you know. In any event, I'd feel honor bound to marry you if *that* ever happened."

"What makes you think I'd want to marry you?"

He shoved her foot into her boot. "Katie, if you ever gave yourself to me it would be because you loved me with all your heart. That's the sort of girl you are. You'd never give your delectable body to a man you did not love. Therefore, if I ever took you to my bed, I'd understand the rules and act accordingly. If I bedded you, I would have to marry you."

He took her other boot. "Give me your foot."

Still yawning, she stuck it out for him.

"You're quite a lump in the morning, aren't you?"

His smile was achingly affectionate, so she could not be angry with him. She laughed softly. "Apparently so. I'm usually an early riser and quite cheerful, but not when awakened this early."

He turned away while she quickly changed shirts. Once she was done, he stuck the cap on her head, then gathered up the two travel pouches and slung them over his shoulder. "Come along, Caleb."

He held out his hand and she simply slipped hers into it without thinking. It felt so natural and right. Heaven help her! She had to be sleep deprived if she ever thought holding Niall's hand felt right.

But it did.

His grasp was warm and comforting, and quite protective in the way his fingers entwined with hers.

"Katie, stop fretting. No one will think twice about it," he said, glancing at their clasped hands. "They all believe you are a simpleton and will expect me to keep hold of you."

"Fine, but if you shout in my face and make those stupid gestures again," she said, mimicking the gestures he'd made yesterday when indicating food and sleep, "I vow I will kick you until your shins bleed. You are having far too much fun at my expense."

He arched an eyebrow, casting her that deliciously wicked smile of his again. "Are you always this much of a growling bear in the morning?"

"You bring out the worst in me." She said nothing more as he opened the door to their bedchamber and led her downstairs to their waiting carriage. She felt their driver's eyes on her, but dared not look up at him for fear of giving herself away.

Perhaps she was merely imagining the shiftiness of his gaze. She would mention it to Niall once they were on their way. In any event, they would be changing horses several times throughout the day. Why not change drivers as well?

Riding in the coach was certainly more convenient, but not more comfortable. The springs were worn and probably had not been very good to begin with even when this conveyance was new. However, to engage a fancier one would attract too much attention. Few people would notice a man and a young boy riding in a careworn carriage.

The rest of the day went smoothly, for the weather held up and the roadways remained dry. They passed through Newcastle without incident and stopped for the night just outside of town at another of the commonly used coaching inns, The Swan and Maiden. It was not among the finest, but their driver had mentioned it was a convenient place to stop for the night.

To Katie, it appeared to be at the lower end of respectability, a little too run down for her liking.

Since it was the coach driver's job to attend to the carriage horses, Katie walked in with Niall, but made sure to remain standing just behind him so that no one had a clear look at her face.

"I'd like a private room," Niall said to the proprietor, striding in as though he owned the place. She supposed this was the manner of all noblemen since they seemed to be privileged in this regard, always getting their way. "It's just me and the boy. We'll also want supper brought up."

She felt the proprietor's gaze on her. "What's wrong with him, my lord?"

Niall remained remarkably calm. "Nothing. Why? He's mute and a little hard of hearing. That's all. This is why he's shy. You'll frighten him if you come near him. He's afraid of strangers, as you can well understand. They often treat him poorly. He is under my protection now and I will not allow him to be taunted or ridiculed."

"Yes, m'lord. But I still must be sure he has no fever. We had a bloke in just yesterday trying to pass off a sick child."

"And you sent them away?" Niall remarked, his anger barely leashed.

"I have an establishment to run. What do you think would happen if all my guests suddenly took ill? Who knows what diseases that child was carrying?" He thumped the guest register closed and came around his desk toward them.

Katie's heart began to pound. What would she do if he ripped off her cap? Or made her look into his eyes?

But Niall seemed not at all concerned, or perhaps he was better at keeping his wits about him than she was.

"Hold on, Mr. Swann," he said to the innkeeper whose name was clearly marked upon a slate board behind his desk.

Katie wondered whether this was really his name or everyone had merely taken to calling him that since the inn's name was The Swan and Maiden.

"As I said," Niall continued, his voice casual and steady, "you'll scare the lad. Let me handle it." He turned to face Katie. "Caleb," he said loudly in her ear, "give me your hand."

Katie held it out tenuously.

"The proprietor is going to feel your skin. Don't be scared. I'm right here with you. He isn't going to hurt you."

Katie silently swore she was going to poke Niall in the nose once they were safely up in their guest chamber. She would indeed be deaf if he kept shouting in her ear. But for now, she did as he asked and held out a trembling hand.

"There," Niall said more gently. "Caleb's skin would be burning if he had a fever. Is that not so, Mr. Swann?"

The proprietor harrumphed. "I suppose. The lad has soft hands."

"He's young still and cannot do much. But he is dear to us and I will be most displeased if anyone here treats him ill. Now, may we have the room?"

"Aye, m'lord. Let me show ye the way up." He turned to summon one of the lads working behind the bar in the common room.

Niall stopped him. "I've got our travel bags. No need to disturb your staff. Just show us to our chamber."

The room had only the one bed, a surprisingly large and comfortable looking one.

Katie tried not to respond with alarm since she would be making a pallet on the floor for herself anyway. Thankfully, no bath was ordered, just food. She crossed the room and pretended to gaze out the window while Mr. Swann spoke to Niall.

She knew the moment Niall tipped the man an extra shilling or two, for his manner suddenly turned obsequious and he could not do enough for them. "And here's a little extra to take care of our coachman."

The man bowed and scraped his way out.

Katie turned to Niall the moment the door closed behind the innkeeper. "Do you think he suspects?"

Niall tossed the travel pouches down on the table. "No. Even if he did, he'll keep his mouth shut for the few extra coins tossed his way. I noticed a newspaper on his desk when we first entered. It's likely several days old, but it had nothing about a runaway bride on the front page."

"Thank goodness. Perhaps only the Bow Street runners know of my disappearance and most of them will be searching in the wrong places."

"Let's hope so."

He removed his jacket and strode to the basin to pour water in it and wash up. But he stopped her when she came over to do the same. "Keep your cap on, Katie. Your jacket, too. One of the inn's staff will be delivering our food. Pretend to still be staring out the window when they walk in. I don't like this place. The coach driver and proprietor have something going on."

"I felt it, too. What do you think they are up to?"

"I'm not sure yet." He moved the lamp off the table and set it on the bureau, intending to keep her away from the glare of illumination. "In any event, they aren't likely to try anything with me. Few people would ever dare incur the wrath of an earl."

"Let's hope so." She was dusty and itchy, wishing she could clean up as he was doing now. But he was right. She could not chance being noticed. "Why did you give the innkeeper a little extra for our driver if you don't trust either of them?"

"It never hurts to spread a little coin here and there."

Although Niall had kept his manner calm when speaking to her, she sensed he was anything but. Her eyes rounded in alarm when he withdrew the pistol he kept hidden in the lip of his boot and checked it before putting it back in place. "We ought to make Thirsk by late tomorrow evening. I know the innkeeper at the Mablethorpe Inn quite well. He'll quietly arrange transportation for us to York."

"Leaving this coachman behind?"

He nodded. "He won't know we've gone until hours later, and he'll believe we've taken the road through Leeds since it's fastest to London."

"Then why shouldn't we take that route?"

"I dare not risk it. That's where the Bow Street runners will be concentrating their efforts. There'll be men watching for us at each coaching inn along the way. We'll head to York instead and lose ourselves in the city for the night. From there, we'll divert our route to a little town on the North Sea called Mablethorpe. It will cause us to lose a day in reaching London, but it's safer than attempting the more direct route."

"Mablethorpe?" She eyed him curiously. "Same name as the inn at Thirsk?"

He nodded. "The innkeeper and his family are from there. His nephews are coach drivers and completely trustworthy. They'll take us to London, keeping to the quieter coast roads."

She cautiously peered out the window to the empty street below. "Are you sure they can be trusted?"

"Yes."

She let out a breath, watching the vapor form against the window pane. "So we just have to get through tonight."

"You can take the bed. I'm not going to sleep."

Now he was scaring her. What had they gotten themselves into? "Not at all? You think they're up to something bad? Why don't we just leave now?"

"No horses or carriages available. It's too late in the evening." He said nothing more, turning to the door when he heard a knock. The proprietor announced he'd brought up their food. "Ah, thank you, Mr. Swann."

The man seemed in no hurry to leave. "What's the lad doing? Doesn't he wish to take off his cap and jacket?"

The man was too nosy by far. Katie feared the trouble was about to start now. But Niall seemed to take it all in stride. "He'll get around to it in his own good time," he said with a good natured chuckle. "This place is new to Caleb and it will take him some time to settle in. He will soon, never you worry. I'm sure he'll enjoy the meal. Good night, Mr. Swann. Make certain our coach is ready to leave at daybreak."

The innkeeper ignored the dismissal and started to approach Katie, but

Niall blocked him. "What is your interest in the boy?" he asked, all pretense at joviality suddenly gone.

"Why, nothing, m'lord."

Even she noticed the uneasy edge to the man's voice, but she simply did not understand what his purpose was.

Niall's voice suddenly turned cold as ice. "If I see you anywhere near Caleb," he said, his tone lethal, "I shall beat you to a bloody pulp and haul your carcass to the local magistrate. Do you understand me?"

The man held up his hands in mock surrender. "I mean him no harm, m'lord. Just trying to be friendly."

"He doesn't need your friendship. Keep away from him. Get out and don't come in here again." He slammed the door shut and latched it, then lifted the bureau and placed it against the door.

"Niall?" She wasn't certain what was happening, only that the innkeeper made her quite uncomfortable. Perhaps they ought to have sought out one of the finer inns even if the risk was greater. "What is going on?"

"You are drawing too much attention."

She groaned. "I knew it. The innkeeper suspects I'm a girl."

"No, Katie. He believes you are a boy. The coachman, too."

"Then where's the problem?"

"I'll explain it to you once we are away from here. Have your supper."

She sat down at the small table and picked up a fork, but her stomach was in too much of a roil to settle down. She ignored the meat pasty and simply ate a little of the bread to hold her over until morning. "I don't have much of an appetite."

Niall strode to her side. "Nor do I. Let's get some sleep. I'll make a pallet for myself beside the hearth."

She swallowed hard. "No, don't bother. Who knows what might crawl over you while you sleep. Take the bed."

"And let you sleep on the floor?" He frowned. "That isn't going to happen, so don't bother arguing about it."

"I won't." She took a deep breath. "We'll share the bed."

Niall appeared to stop breathing.

"It is the only sensible thing to do. And we'll both stay fully dressed. Besides, the bed is big enough to accommodate two. We'll easily fit without having to lay on top of each other. Just keep to your side and I'll keep to mine."

"That is a very bad idea."

"What? Keeping to our own sides? Or sharing the bed?" She sighed and shook her head. "Don't you turn priggish on me. As you've pointed out, I've already ruined myself by running off. Now I am traveling to London alone with you. Sharing the bed will add nothing more to the damage I've done to myself. Just keep your hands off me and we'll be fine."

He ignored her and made a pallet for himself on the floor.

"I see," she said in a broken whisper, realizing their developing friendship was all in her imagination. She'd thought it was turning into something more than friendship, to be truthful. But he did not feel the same.

This wicked earl, who had the reputation of never turning a woman away from his bed, had just openly and firmly refused her. It was humiliating. She wasn't even asking for them to do anything more than sleep.

Why did he dislike her so much?

CHAPTER NINE

B ETWEEN HIS BODY'S savage desire for Katie, and his uneasiness about the innkeeper and the coachman, Niall did not manage a wink of sleep the entire night. It mattered little since he'd make up for it later in the coach, but he was riled and exhausted, and those were not a good combination.

He needed to keep his wits about him, at least until they were safely on the road again.

"Katie," he whispered, shaking her gently to wake her. The sky had turned gray with the approaching dawn and he did not wish to lose another moment of time.

"It cannot be dawn yet."

"It is, love." *Bollocks*. He hadn't meant to use the endearment. For all his lecturing about her keeping to her Caleb disguise, he was the one who needed the reminder most.

She snuffled, obviously having fallen back to sleep.

He shook her again, trying to ignore the heat shooting through his body as he put his hands on her warm, little body. Her sweet face was peeking out from under the covers. He did not think a more beautiful girl existed.

What was happening to him?

She'd gone to bed last night believing he did not like her.

Hah! That pendulum had swung hard in the opposite direction. He used to think of her as an irritatingly priggish miss who always showed him up with her perfect manners and perfectly complacent ways. But now?

Yes, she was still perfect. Lovely and engaging, compassionate and clever. He knew exactly what was happening to him.

He was falling in love with Katie.

Not merely falling, but tumbling, careening, diving headlong into love with her.

It was a frightening feeling.

He'd never felt so out of control before, so desperately famished for any woman or so afraid of losing his heart.

What a jest, a Jameson desiring a deep and committed lifetime love.

But how could he be certain these feelings he had for Katie would last? After all, he came from a long bloodline of cads and heels. What if he returned to his womanizing ways?

Katie was the last person on earth he would ever wish to destroy.

He was distracted from his musings by the sound of their coach being brought around to the front. He left Katie's side to peer out the window and saw the coachman speaking to the innkeeper, Swann. By their intense manner, they seemed to be plotting something, not merely holding idle conversation.

When they both looked up at his window, he knew what they meant to do. He'd drawn back before they noticed him, but this did not give him much advantage. "Katie, get up. *Now.*"

The urgency in his voice finally roused her. She shot out of bed and hastily donned her boots, jacket and cap. "What's wrong?"

"You do not leave my side even for a moment. Got it?"

She nodded. "I suppose that means I cannot kick you out of here while I use..." She glanced toward the chamber pot.

He sighed. "I'll turn around. Be quick about it."

He returned to staring out the window. Once she had finished and washed up, he gathered their pouches, took her hand, and led her downstairs. The innkeeper was waiting for them by the door. "My lord, may I have just a moment of your time? It won't take long. The lad can wait in the coach."

"No, Mr. Swann." He held fast to Katie, knowing his grip was tight. But no one was going to pry her away from him. "I know what your game is. If you or the coachman set a hand on the boy I shall see you both hanged."

He then turned to the coachman who was standing beside their coach. "Step away."

"What do ye mean, m'lord?"

"You are not driving us anywhere. Hitch a ride on the next coach heading south. You will find your coach and horses waiting for you at the next inn on the route."

"Now see here! That's thievery!"

He grabbed the man by the lapels and tossed him toward the innkeeper. "There is no theft involved. I've paid you for coach transportation to Thirsk. I've paid you for your services as driver, as well. Obviously, I cannot allow you to continue. If anything, you owe me my money back. Caleb, climb up in the driver's seat." He shoved Katie up there none too gently and climbed up beside her. "Good day, gentlemen."

Katie said nothing, merely stared at him with mouth agape until they were out of sight of the inn. "Will you now tell me what that was about?"

"No."

She gave a startled laugh. "Why ever not?"

"Because it is an ugly business." Lord, he was still angry over the encounter. Seething, actually. It was one thing for consenting adults to do as they wished between themselves, but to take advantage of a child? This is what these men had wanted to do with Katie, believing her to be a simple-minded boy who would not be able to understand what those friendly pats and other touches were about. Nor would a mute boy be able to shout for help even if he did understand.

Such things happened all the time. Worse things happened to unprotected children, girls sold to rookeries, boys doing whatever they needed to survive on the streets. Too often, those in power would do nothing to prevent it, sometimes even offering protection for those who ran these sordid establishments.

But to dare attempt this on a child under an earl's protection? It made no sense, unless…

Oh, lord! They'd thought he was one of them!

Katie cried out as the coach sped over a particularly rough patch of terrain. "Niall! The coach is going to tip over if you drive these horses any faster. What is wrong with you?"

It took him another long moment to calm down, but his ire finally began to subside and he slowed the horses to a more moderate pace. He was still too agitated to talk about her close call with those fiends calmly, so he ignored the question when she asked it again.

He knew he was behaving like an arse, but she seemed to sense his turmoil and take it with remarkable patience. "I can't yet, Katie. We'll talk about it once we're settled in our room at Thirsk, all right?"

She nodded.

They rode on in silence.

The weather was turning cool and damp, the sign of an approaching storm. He could smell it in the salty air, for storms had a slightly acrid, metallic scent to them, especially the more violent ones, as he feared this one would be.

He hoped they would reach Thirsk before the deluge came upon them.

They stopped briefly at the next coaching inn along the route, just long enough to have a quick bite, drop off the horses and coach, and pick up fresh horses for themselves. It would be faster if they rode on horseback to Thirsk rather than hire another coach.

They did make good time, but were caught in the downpour on the outskirts of town and soaked to the bone by the time they reached the Mablethorpe Inn. Mr. Mablethorpe was standing at the porticoed entrance as they rode up. "Lord Jameson! We did not expect to see you."

"Nor did I expect to be here again so soon. We are drenched and in need of a room, your finest if it is available," he said, dismounting and attempting to shake the excess water off him, like a dog after a swim in a lake.

"Yes, of course." He whistled for one of his stable hands to grab the horses. "And who is this fine lad?"

Katie was still seated upon her horse, still hesitant to climb down.

Niall was reluctant to lie to the innkeeper, for he was an excellent man and could be trusted with the secret of her identity. But he was not going to reveal to the truth to him while out in the open and guests milling about in the entry hall. "His name is Caleb. He is mute and slightly hard of hearing. A grandson of the Crisps. Do you recall my caretaker and his wife? I'm delivering him back to his parents in London."

"Yes, lovely people." He waved to Katie and cast her a friendly smile. "Hello there, little fellow! Oh, the poor lad appears exhausted."

"We've had a long ride." He helped Katie dismount, frowning when he felt her legs begin to buckle.

"The lad seems awfully timid, almost scared."

"Yes, we hit a spot of trouble at The Swan and Maiden last night." He kept hold of Katie, worried that he'd pushed her too hard. They'd left at dawn and it was now well after sundown. They'd had another difficult day and they were both drenched.

Mr. Mablethorpe muttered an oath. "That filthy place? How did ye end up there?" He studied Katie and frowned. "Ye didn't leave the boy alone with–"

"No, I quickly saw what they were about. I see you have a fire going in the common room." He would carry Katie inside if he had to, the hell with deception. But she recovered quickly and turned away to busy herself by unbuckling their travel pouches.

She attempted to sling them over her shoulder as she'd seen him do, but her shoulders were quite slender and the pouches were heavier than she expected. The weight of them knocked her backward as she tossed them over her shoulder. Niall caught her in time to keep her from tumbling. "Let me have them, Caleb."

But Katie was not giving them up. When she recovered her balance and finally got them on her shoulder, they slipped right off.

"The lad's not too bright in the head, is he yer lordship?" the innkeeper said in a whisper, obviously not realizing Katie could hear every word.

"He's a good lad. He tries his best." Chuckling, Niall took the pouches from her, tossed them over his shoulder with no effort at all, and returned his attention to the innkeeper. "We'll need food brought up to our chamber. Neither of us has eaten much today."

"At once, m'lord." He smiled at Katie, who was trying to hide herself behind Niall's broad back. But Mr. Mablethorpe was determined to be kind to her. "Food!" he cried, shouting in poor Katie's ear and patting his hand in a circle on his own stomach to assure her it would be delicious. "And a warm bath!" He danced around, mimicking washing his body with a sponge.

Niall was not sure how much longer Katie could keep up the pretense. Her lips were twitching and all would be lost if she broke out in laughter. Well, there would be little harm done. The man and his family were to be trusted.

Indeed, Niall should have revealed the truth and asked for separate quarters. But he could not bring himself to be separated from Katie.

As she'd said often enough, she was ruined anyway. Sleeping apart would not restore her reputation. Nor would he catch a wink of sleep worrying about her if she was not in sight of him.

They went inside while one of the stable hands took their horses to be fed and properly tended. Niall tossed the lad a coin for his efforts.

"What a difference from one inn to the other," Katie whispered while the friendly Mr. Mablethorpe ran inside ahead of them, shouting orders to his staff. The place was well maintained and spotless. The guests were also of a higher class, families traveling with children. Gentlemen discussing business transactions over glasses of brandy.

The aroma of fresh coffee and warm pie filled the air.

The innkeeper's wife rushed out of the kitchen and, clucking like a mother hen, nudged them toward the warming fire in the common room.

"Ye poor lad," she said to Katie, who was clutching her cap and holding it down before the well-meaning proprietress could take it off her.

"The boy is shy," Niall said, not liking to lie to the amiable woman. But there were other diners in the common room and he could not risk Katie's identity being discovered here. "Let him be. I'll take care of him once we are shown to our room."

"Boy? My arse," the woman said, obviously shocking Katie. But she had the sense to keep her voice down and not say another word until they were taken up to their guest chamber. Then, the proprietress closed the door and folded her beefy arms across her ample chest. "Yer lordship, with all due respect, we are running a reputable establishment here."

Niall rubbed a hand across the back of his neck. "Nor will I give you cause to regret giving this room to me and…Caleb."

The woman rolled her eyes. "Who are ye, lass?"

Niall did not allow Katie to answer. "Bring up the latest newspaper, Mrs. Mablethorpe, and I shall tell you. I must also beg you and your husband not to give us away, or you'll put the lass in grave danger."

"Danger?" She lumbered to Katie and tucked a finger under her chin to raise Katie's gaze to hers. "What a sweet thing ye are. Who would want to harm an angel like yerself?" She gave a tsk and hurried out to fetch the paper, returning with it and Mr. Mablethorpe at her heels.

"Yer food and bath will be brought up shortly," he said, closing the door before he went to the hearth to light the fire. "What's all this about, yer lordship?"

Niall took a moment to look at the front page and saw the news had finally made the headlines. He cast Katie a grim smile. "Word is now out. Ten thousand pounds reward offered by your father. An equal sum to be matched by Yardsley."

"Oh, no." She came to his side and read over his arm. "Twenty thousand pounds? Everyone in England will be looking for me now."

Mr. Mablethorpe glanced up in surprise. "The boy speaks? I thought ye said he was mute."

His wife rapped him on the head. "Idiot, does she look like a boy? Ye're looking at Miss Pringle."

His eyes widened in understanding. "The runaway bride?"

Katie took the wet cap off her head. "Yes, but I will never marry Lord Yardsley now. He is a horrible, wretched man."

"Aren't they all?" intoned Mrs. Mablethorpe. "But Lord Jameson's right nice. Ye like him, don't ye? Is this why ye ran off? Ye realized yer heart was bound to him and not Yardsley?"

Niall grimaced. "Not like that at all. Katie, may I tell them?"

She nodded. "Why not? I'm sure all my friends suspect what happened anyway. I was the only fool who remained blind to their deceit."

"She caught Yardsley, the bastard, doing the deed with her best friend moments before they were to marry."

"In the church, no less," Katie added, as though it made a difference where the pair cheated.

"The unfaithful wretch!" Mrs. Mablethorpe was aghast.

"So I ran off. I'd made it as far as Alnwick when I almost drowned in a river. Lord Jameson rescued me and he is now trying to return me safely to my father. But with this reward…everyone will be out hunting for me. The more desperate ones will think nothing of harming Lord Jameson or anyone else who gets in their way."

"This is why Miss Pringle needs to remain in disguise." Niall cleared his throat. "And she also needs to remain with me so I may continue to protect her."

"And claim the reward," the innkeeper interjected.

Katie gasped. "No, he doesn't want it. Although I've told him not to be stupid and take every last ha'penny of it. Whatever my fate, it would not hurt so much if I knew that a fine man such as Lord Jameson had come out ahead in this sad affair. Don't you think he ought to take it, Mrs. Mablethorpe? Surely you can understand why I would be distressed if he did not."

The woman glanced from Katie to him and smiled. "Oh, I understand." She lumbered to Katie's side and patted her hand. "We're not going to give ye away, m'darling."

"Thank you," Katie said, her smile stealing Niall's breath away.

Mrs. Mablethorpe patted her hand once more before starting for the door. "Ye just make yerselves comfortable while we bring up yer meal and bath. Ye can hang yer wet clothes on the pegs along the mantel. They'll dry quick enough as the room warms."

She was still chattering instructions as she and her husband walked out.

Niall closed the door and securely latched it. Not that there was cause for worry here. The innkeeper's wife was hopelessly romantic, perhaps even more so than Katie. The husband was more pragmatic. He'd pay the man a share of the reward, assuming he decided to claim it, if it was necessary to buy his silence. He did not think it would be, for his wife would do the man bodily harm if he dared ask for so much as a shilling from him.

Years ago he'd saved the life of one of their sons when their stable had caught fire. A frightened horse had kicked over the lamp the boy had set too close on the ground. Being young himself, he'd never considered his own mortality, and went running in upon hearing the boy's screams.

While he had been busy saving young Douglas Mablethorpe and the horse he had been tending, the other stable hands had managed to get the other horses out in time. The incident had left him with a slight burn scar on his left shoulder that was hardly noticeable now.

"Come stand by the hearth, Katie. Give me your cap and jacket. I'll hang them up."

She did as he asked, remaining beside him as they held their hands close to the flames to warm them. "Do you think they might have robes for us to borrow? Everything we're wearing is soaked. So are the clothes in the pouches. I had better hang them up to dry, too."

"I'll help you." Because if he did not keep busy, he was going to kiss her. There was something exquisite about this girl. The way she was put together. Big eyes. Softest lips. Pert nose and pink cheeks. Dark hair. Stunning body. Even when soaking wet and obviously bedraggled, she looked beautiful.

They made quick work of hanging up the clothes from the pouch, but they could not take off more than their boots and stockings. The boots were left beside the fire. He placed her stockings on a peg beside the cap and jacket she had earlier removed and put to dry above the mantel.

He would have preferred for them not to remain in their wet shirts and breeches, but they could not stand naked beside each other. Well, he could. He did not care.

But Katie was modest.

Biblical plagues would fall upon them before Katie ever stripped for him and strutted about the chamber without any clothes on.

Oddly, that modesty made her all the more tempting to him.

"May I unpin my hair?" she asked. "I've been wearing it tightly done up and it's hurting my head."

"Yes, of course. No need for deception now. Let me help you." He felt her shiver as his fingers grazed her neck. His hands were cold, but not that cold. He knew she was responding to the pleasure of his touch. He was no less immune to her, and in fact was probably in great danger of doing something foolish. The intimacy between them felt particularly intense after the ugliness of last night's lodgings and this morning's confrontation.

"Thank you," she said, her voice soft and shaking as he took out the last of the hair pins.

He moved away to place them atop the bureau and regain control of his pounding heart.

How was he going to get through the night without kissing her? He wanted to do more, of course. Mere kisses would never be enough.

"This guest chamber is so lovely, don't you think so Niall?" She shook her hair out, not realizing the effect it was having on him as it tumbled down her back like a waterfall of dark silk.

"Yes, charming. Stay by the fire. I don't want you to catch a chill." Or be anywhere near him while his heart was untamed and on a rampage of desire.

The room was well appointed and far too cosy for his liking. The heat from the fire now chased the dampness from the air. It made for a romantic atmosphere. But he supposed being anywhere with Katie would make him feel this way.

Her eyes were closed and she looked beautiful beyond imagination. "I wish they'd bring the food up. I'm starved. Aren't you?"

"Yes, Katie. You have no idea how famished I am." He was speaking of her, of course. Nothing was going to satisfy that hunger.

She laughed, a soft, musical trill. "Although I think I'd much rather have the bath first. I stink of horse sweat and saddle leather."

"You? Never. You are a rose blossom."

She opened her eyes and smiled at him. "And I think you are delirious."

After a moment, she began to nibble her lip. "Niall, what are we going to do for clothes? Ours are all wet and Mrs. Mablethorpe did not mention providing any for us while ours dry. We ought to have mentioned it to her while she was in here."

Was Katie just realizing it now? He'd been thinking of nothing else for the past few minutes. "We'll say something about it when she or her husband returns."

He did not require clothes, just a drying cloth or spare sheet to tuck around his waist for the sake of Katie's modesty.

Otherwise, he would not care who saw him undressed.

But Katie was going to bite through her lip, she was that appalled by the situation. She would never agree to toss a sheet around her luscious body.

Blessed saints! He'd be lost if she ever did.

How would he resist such a sight? Katie gift wrapped for him, those big eyes of hers looking up at him, her long hair tumbling over her bare shoulders. Hound that he was, he'd have her naked in a trice.

The way she had been looking at him lately, he did not think she would resist.

This was bad.

Fiery desire had been building between them since she'd arrived at Alnwick. Merely a simmer, at first. But over the past few days it had been bubbling. Brewing. Tonight it would spill over and burn both of them.

Were it any other woman, he would already be taking advantage. Of course, the women who ended up in his bed – or he in theirs – were never virgins. They were elegant courtesans, sophisticated women, wealthy widows, or married noblewomen whose husbands cared little what their wives did so long as they were discreet about it.

But Katie was different.

She was an angel.

If he touched her, he would have to marry her. And if he married her, he would have to take his wedding vows seriously, be faithful to her, love and protect her to his dying breath. She deserved no less.

He turned away to dig into his travel pouch and remove his comb. "Here. You'll need to brush out your hair."

But he dared not remain beside her beyond handing her the comb because his fingers were itching to slide through those silken strands.

He crossed to the window and stared into oblivion.

Rain pelted the panes and the wind howled against them, causing them to rattle violently. After several minutes, he drew over a stool and sank onto it, resting his elbows on his thighs and staring at the floor.

Anything to avoid looking at Katie.

Her beauty overwhelmed him.

His desire for her was as fierce as the storm raging outside.

"Niall, what's wrong?"

He gave a mirthless laugh. "Nothing."

He felt her silence, just as he had felt hers.

He also felt the force of her gaze on him. He glanced up and saw she was still watching him, her expression thoughtful. He arched an eyebrow. "What?"

"Nothing," she said, tossing the word back at him.

"Truly, Katie. What is it? I know you have something on your mind. You look troubled."

"We both seem to be, don't we?" But she nodded and did not press him further. "I'm not troubled so much as confused. I'm trying to make sense of it, but the answer escapes me. Perhaps the answer is obvious, but it's hurtful. So I don't want to accept it."

"Tell me what has you bedeviled." He meant it sincerely, for he never wanted Katie to be afraid to share her feelings with him.

Her expression turned pained. "It concerns you."

He crossed to her side, knowing he should not get anywhere near this girl who was so dangerous to his heart. "All the more reason you should confide in me."

Tears formed in her eyes. "Why would you not share the bed with me last night?"

CHAPTER TEN

NIALL DID NOT know whether to laugh or groan at Katie's question. "Share a bed? Do you hear yourself? What a question to ask a renowned rake. Why do you think I refused?"

The breath caught in her throat and her lovely lips began to quiver. "Because you do not find me attractive."

He heard the little catch of heartbreak in her voice and it tore him to pieces. Is this truly what she believed?

"Shows what you know about men," he grumbled, wishing they were not engaging in this conversation. Where were the Mablethorpes when he needed them? And the food? Or the bath?

"What do you mean?"

"If I did not like you, I'd have you out of your clothes and romping in that bed with me right now."

"You'd have me…if you did not like me?" She frowned. "That makes no sense whatsoever."

"It makes perfect sense. You are not any man's plaything, Katie. Taking you to bed would have to be a declaration of love on my part."

She nodded. "And you don't love me."

"Don't put words in my mouth. All I'm saying is that I could never bed you and then leave you. My conscience would not allow it. Yet, it is not in my nature to remain faithful to one woman."

"Because you are a Jameson bee and this is what they do?"

He regarded her, confused. "A what?"

"A Jameson bee. Like your father and grandfather before you."

"I still have no clue what you are talking about."

"You flit from flower to flower, steal their pollen, and then move on to the next flower and steal her pollen."

"I am not a damn bee."

"The point is, what you are telling me is that you won't touch me because I am the foolish sort of girl who requires a lifetime commitment, and you are the sort of man who is incapable of giving it."

"I–" A knock at their door interrupted their conversation. It was probably for the best. He was moments away from declaring his love for her and that would be an enormous mistake. As she had just said, Jamesons were flitting bees who did not know how to be faithful to one flower.

He strode to the door. "Who's there?"

"Mr. Mablethorpe, m'lord."

Niall opened it and allowed the innkeeper to march in with a rolling cart laden with food, ale, and a pitcher of mulled wine. By the heavenly scents, he knew they were in for one of Mrs. Mablethorpe's finest meals. "Is that roast beef she's made for us?"

"Yes, m'lord." His eyes sought Katie who had tucked herself behind the open door on the chance others were in the hall. "Oh, there ye are Miss–"

"Caleb," Niall blurted, frowning at the man. In truth, his wife was the brains in that marriage. Mablethorpe was not nearly as sharp.

Niall hoped he had not made a mistake in confiding in the man.

"Right! My mistake, m'lord. I'll leave ye to it and I'll bring up the tub in half an hour. Perhaps *Caleb* can tuck himself in bed at that time," he said with an exaggerated wink. "I'll require help from some of my lads and we don't want them taking too close a look at…*Caleb*. Does that suit ye?"

Niall sighed. "Yes, thank you for the warning."

He nudged the man out of the room and latched the door behind him. "I'm sorry, Katie. I hope he shuts up about us."

"Nothing we can do about it now. It was bound to happen sooner or later. His wife caught on at once. Hopefully, no one else noticed."

He set out their plates and piled roast beef, a mash of onions and potatoes, and a Yorkshire pudding onto both. "Most of the other guests have turned in for the night," he said, pouring an ale for himself and a cup of the mulled wine for her. "Mablethorpe will have no one to blab to but his wife."

"And his staff, those not yet retired for the evening."

"His wife will make sure he and their workers keep their mouths shut. This is a family run operation. The few on the staff who are outsiders would have gone home by now. Those who are on duty this evening and might have seen us will be Mablethorpe relations. They will never betray us." He set out a chair for her. "Come have a bite."

She sank into the chair and immediately reached for her cup of mulled wine. She must have been very thirsty, for she gulped down the entire contents. "Katie! Don't drink it so fast."

"This is remarkably good." She held out her cup so he could pour more into it.

He frowned when she cast him a tipsy looking smile, knowing it had already gone to her head. Well, her nerves were frayed and she though he did not like her. She was overset. But he would watch her and make certain she did not imbibe too much. He refused to consider what might happen with her inhibitions loosened.

He made sure she ate something before he refilled her cup which was already empty again. Was she purposely trying to make herself drunk? Not that he blamed her. He'd been on the run with her for a couple of days. She'd been on the run for over a week now.

The wear on her senses, especially for someone as sheltered as she had always been, must be something awful.

She had just stuffed a spoonful of the onion and potato mash in her mouth when she suddenly groaned. "Oh, no."

"What is it, Katie?" She looked like a very sad kitten.

"We forgot to ask for clothes." She let out her breath in a groan. "What are we going to do?"

He'd been so concerned about keeping Mablethorpe in line he'd completely forgotten about requesting them. But the man would be back soon to retrieve the empty plates and bring up their bath. The oversight was nothing dire.

But Katie had imbibed too much and was not thinking clearly.

The look of dismay on her face had him grinning. "Oh, dear. What a coil. This is a disaster of catastrophic proportions."

"It is. You have no idea." She poured herself more mulled wine and took a healthy swig that would have made a sailor proud. "What I think…" She hiccuped. "Obviously, the only sensible thing…"

He stopped her when she reached for more. "I think you've had enough."

She tossed her table linen at him. "This is my adventure, not yours."

He nodded. "But we don't want you getting too adventurous and regretting it later, do we?"

She looked down at her clasped hands.

He took hold of them, lightly caressing them with the soft swirl of his thumbs. "Katie, are you all right?"

"No, I'm not." Her eyes began to tear. "My feeling are in such turmoil.

Now I'm going to make an utter cake of myself. But I don't care. I've made myself too drunk to care. Anyway, it cannot be worse than the ruined laughingstock everyone in London already believes me to be." She took a deep, shattered breath. "We've been found out and my adventure will soon be over. This is the most fun I've had in my entire life. No one has ever made me as happy as you do."

"Oh, Katie..."

"But it's more than that. You act like a rogue, but this is not who you truly are. You are brave and caring."

He snorted. "No one's ever called me that."

She tossed him an endearingly lopsided smile. "They've never had the pleasure of being on the run with you as I have. I feel safe with you. And do not deny that you are brave because I won't believe otherwise. I'm not sure what was going on with those nasty men at last night's inn, but you knew they were up to something unsavory and protected me."

He would have killed them if they'd ever laid a hand on her.

"But it isn't just about your valor. You also know how to enjoy life, to laugh and be silly, to find pleasure in everything you do. You've always been this way and I've always loved watching you. Finally, I got to share in the fun with you and I've treasured every moment."

She overwhelmed him, demolished each and every one of his defenses. "As I have with you, Katie. I want you to know this."

"You are merely being polite. I'm so pathetic, not even a wicked earl like you will have me in his bed."

He stared at her with his mouth agape. "I've told you why. It isn't about not wanting you."

"I know. It's about not wanting me permanently." She nodded. "Much as I've tried, I have not drunk myself into oblivion yet. So I understand perfectly what is going on. But you do not seem to be getting my point."

It was hard to pay attention to her words when all he wanted to do was kiss her daintily pursed lips.

Were sweeter lips ever created?

Or a more beautiful face?

The wine had turned her nose and cheeks a bright pink. Her eyes were glistening. Her lips were cherry red and her expression resembled something between a sensual pout and a lopsided grin. He found it surprisingly seductive. "And what is your point?"

He was struggling not to devour her.

But she ravaged his senses and left him famished, starved for the littlest morsel of her.

She eased out of his grasp and drank more of her mulled wine. "I am setting no terms. I want to be like the others. I do not wish to remain the untouchable Perfect Miss Pringle. I wish to be touched." She paused and scratched her head. "I'm not sure that came out right. What I am trying to tell you, rather inelegantly, is that I am just a woman with an aching heart who wants to spend one night with you. No continuing responsibilities on your part."

He stopped her when she tried to pour herself more wine. "You are going to pass out if you don't stop this nonsense."

She folded her arms on the table, buried her face in them, and began to cry. A few strands of her hair fell into her mash of potatoes. He said nothing for the longest moment, then threw his head back and laughed.

She thought he was being cruel, but he was not.

This is what it took for him to realize what a fool he'd been. He was nothing like the other Jameson men. He was never going to stray. He loved Katie, utterly and irrevocably. How could he possibly ever love anyone else?

He bent on one knee. "Katie, look at me."

"No, you are laughing at me. I've made a fool of myself. I thought I was drunk enough not to care, but it seems I am not."

"Please, love. Look at me." He intended to propose to her...never mind about Yardsley, he'd deal with that hound later. But he'd have to take Katie north to Scotland in order to elope with her. And here they'd spent the past few days riding hard southward. He ought to have listened to his heart sooner and proposed to her from the first.

She was too busy crying to notice what he was doing. "Katie, will you–"

A sharp banging at their door startled both of them.

Hell and damnation.

Was Mablethorpe back already?

He wanted to shout at him to leave the tub and buckets, and go away, but this was no gentle pounding.

Nor had anyone called out to identify themselves.

Whoever was at their door could not be Mablethorpe.

Niall shot to his feet and crossed the room to withdraw the pistol from his boot. He then shoved his feet into the boots, grabbed hers along with the garments drying by the fire, and then hurried back to her side. "Quick, Katie. Put these on."

She wiped her tears with the table linen and hurried to do as he asked. He noticed she'd grabbed her eating knife and now had it grasped in her hand. But he knew she was too softhearted to ever use it.

"Lord Jameson, we know you have her! Open up!"

"Bloody hell, it's those Bow Street men who were watching for you at Alnwick. Digby and Standish. They've caught up to us. Now they've alerted the entire inn." He opened the window, ignoring the blast of cold air and pelting rain that struck him. "We'll have to climb out. Be careful, the roof will be slippery. Stay close and keep hold of me. I won't let you fall."

She hiccuped.

Oh, lord. She was drunk. Even her shirt and jacket were buttoned wrong, but there was no time to fix them now. "Never mind. I'll hold on to you. Just try not to pass out."

"Why would I pass out?"

"Cold air can do that to you. It ferments in your system." He grabbed her by the waist, climbed out the window, and prayed she would not scream as they slid down the roof. He angled his body so that if he fell as they landed on the rain soaked ground, she would safely fall atop him and not the other way around.

Fortunately, they managed to land without either of them falling or twisting an ankle. Since the rain was coming down too hard to talk over it, he simply hauled her over his shoulder and ran to the stables. "Katie, climb up to the loft."

"Why?"

"For pity's sake, don't ask questions. Just do it. Here, I'll help you." He lifted her up, giving her backside a shove upward to set her safely in the loft. She kicked some loosely strewn hay down on his head as she scrambled to hide.

"Sorry," she called down, her face peeking out from behind a bale of hay while she watched him grab their two horses and lead them out of their stalls. He gave each of them a slap on the rump just as an angry roar thundered overhead and a clap of lightning caused the ground to sizzle beneath his boots.

The beasts took off in panic.

He expected they would eventually return to the stable or just gallop to the next coaching inn, for they were used to the route. But he wasted no time speculating. Instead, he hoisted himself into the loft and pulled Katie down next to him just as the Bow Street men ran in.

The older Bow Street man, Charles Digby, kicked the wooden slats in one of the stalls. "Damn, their horses are gone."

"I told you I saw them ride off," said the younger runner, Harlan

Standish. "What do we do now?"

"We follow them, of course," Digby said, emitting a string of curses as he led their skittish horses out of the stable and into the pouring rain. Their beasts had not yet been unsaddled, so they merely climbed on and hurried away.

Niall listened for the clop of hooves to fade away to be sure the Bow Street men were truly gone.

He was not a praying man, but he was praying hard right now that he'd succeeded in leading them on a wild and fruitless chase. "I think it's safe now, Katie. Let me help you down."

She waited for him to swing down and then she lowered herself so he could catch her. "We're soaking wet again," she muttered as he held her in his arms.

"It appears so. And may I say, the look suits you." He tried to concentrate on their next plan and not on her delectable body which really was impossibly distracting.

"What do we do now, Niall?"

"We return to the inn. It ought to be safe enough since the Bow Street men think we've run off. The Mablethorpes will give us another room. Obviously, we cannot go back to the fine one we had. A pity, it was quite nice."

"I feel terrible about what happened. Those awful men broke down the door. Who knows what else they destroyed while chasing us?"

"The Mablethorpes know I will make it right. Don't fret, Katie. They'll hide us elsewhere."

"You'll make it right? No, this is my fault." Her eyes rounded in surprise. "And what makes you think they won't be furious and turn us away?"

"In this storm? They won't. They wouldn't do it even if the day was sunny and warm."

"You're awfully sure of them. Why do you trust them as you do?"

"It's a long story."

"Another long story? I am keeping track. You'll have lots to tell me when we have the chance to talk. When do you think that might be?"

"Later." He kept his arm around her as they ran toward the servants entrance. The door was unlatched, as he hoped it would be.

Mrs. Mablethorpe was waiting for them with a shotgun aimed at the door when they entered. She set it down as soon as she recognized them. "Ye poor lass. Is this what ye've been dealing with since running off?"

Katie nodded. "I'm so sorry for the damage. I'll repay you for all of it.

The room, the meal, the broken door. The trouble I've caused."

Niall frowned at her. "Mrs. Mablethorpe will not accept it. The payment will come from me."

Katie scowled at him. "You? Haven't you sacrificed enough for me?"

"Not nearly enough." He pulled her inside and shut the door behind them. "Is there someplace you can hide us, Mrs. Mablethorpe? Katie is exhausted. So am I."

"And our clothes are soaked again," Katie said, wringing water from her shirt into a nearby bucket.

"I have just the spot. Follow me, my loves." She took them up the back stairs used by her staff and led them to what appeared to be nothing but a wall. "The inn has been around a long time. This secret room was something of a necessity during more turbulent times. We've hidden Yorkist sympathizers and Lancastrians as well. Spies. Smugglers. Royalists. Reformists. Even a queen once, I've been told. It's always kept at the ready."

As she spoke, she moved a small table containing a vase with a large floral display. Niall helped her set it aside. Then she slid her hand behind a nearby wall sconce, and a part of the wall suddenly opened up with a soft *whoosh*. A hidden door. "We cannot roll a tub in here, but I expect you've taken in quite enough water tonight. I'll grab the ewer and basin from the other room for ye. The soap and wash cloths, too. Do ye need any more food?"

"I don't think so, Mrs. Mablethorpe," Katie said, looking to him for approval. "We had just finished our delicious meal when those Bow Street men started pounding on our door."

Niall considered asking for dry clothes, but something stopped him. Perhaps it was the knowledge that he was about to pledge his heart and soul to Katie. He wanted to be left alone with her already.

No more fuss.

No more delays.

He kept silent as the proprietress lit several candles in the room.

He quickly inspected their surroundings, noting the shutters sealed tight and the neatly made up bed designed to fit two people in it. There was a fireplace and wood in a bin beside it. "May I light a fire?"

"Oh, yes. It's quite safe to do so, m'lord. I'll see if I can scrounge up some dry clothes for ye. Let me gather some items and sneak back here before others are alerted to your presence."

"Haven't they been already?" Katie asked. "I mean, surely those Bow Street men created quite an uproar. Everyone will have heard them."

She waved her hand in dismissal. "If a guest asks, we'll give him a drink on the house and apologize for the disruption of those rowdy guests. We'll explain it was all a mistake and the bounders are now gone. No names mentioned. Not yours or theirs. No one will ever know you were here or are still here. One of my sons is a coachman. He'll stop by tomorrow evening and drive you the rest of the way to London. He's a good boy. Size of an ox. No one is going to get the better of him. He can be trusted. He's the one you rescued years ago, m'lord."

"Douglas?" Niall nodded. "Sounds perfect. I had planned on diverting our route and riding to the town of Mablethorpe to engage one of your relations for just this purpose. This will save us the trip."

"Glad we can be of help. I'll bring ye up what items ye'll need for tonight. When ye wake up tomorrow morning, just tug on this rope and one of us will bring up yer breaksfast. Never ye worry, I'll not leave ye to starve."

She skittered out of the room, returning several minutes later with ewer and basin in hand, and an enormous robe that would easily wrap four times around Katie. "Well, that should do it. Good evening, my lord." She nodded toward Katie and smiled. "And to ye, my lady."

Niall grinned once they were finally left to themselves.

Katie shook her head. "Why did she address me as 'my lady' when she must know I'm only Miss Pringle?"

"You'll soon be a lady, she expects."

She frowned. "Never! I am not going to marry Yardsley and no one can ever make me."

"She wasn't referring to Yardsley." He strode to the hearth, began to place logs one atop the other, and then placed kindling beneath the piled logs in order to start the blaze. They were soaked to the skin again and dripping everywhere.

Since he was starting to feel the cold, he knew Katie had to be freezing. Yet, she hadn't complained. In truth, she hadn't complained about anything the entire journey.

How had he been such an arse about her all these years?

He waited to be sure the wood caught flame before setting aside the fire iron and striding to her side.

He could see the little pulse at the base of her neck rapidly beating. She looked up at him with big, hopeful eyes. "Who does she think I am going to marry?"

CHAPTER ELEVEN

NIALL WAS ASTOUNDED by how unaware Katie was of her allure. "Mrs. Mablethorpe thinks you are going to marry me, of course."

"Why would she think that?" Her eyes grew wide. "Would you ever have me? You never liked me."

"The young Niall Jameson was too much of an idiot ever to appreciate you. But I like to think I've grown wiser with age. Much wiser." He caressed her cheek. "I love you, Katie Pringle. I think you are the only one who hasn't realized it yet."

Bollocks.

She was going to cry again.

She turned away with a sob and buried her hands in her face. "Don't say it unless you mean it, Niall. If I allow myself to fall in love with you, I'll never be able to stop loving you. Not even when you leave me for those fast women in London. I'll pine for you and wither like a dying flower on a vine."

He rolled his eyes. "I am never going to stop loving you."

He wanted to punch Yardsley for beating her down so badly, and berate her parents for caring so much what others thought, that they'd almost crushed the spirit out of her. Nor could he ever forgive himself for behaving like an utter braying donkey around her all these years.

"How can you be certain you will always love me?" She turned to look at him with her big, beautiful eyes.

"Because your nose turns bright pink when you are drunk. And you still have a bit of potato in your hair. Wet hay, too." He removed a few blades of hay as he brushed the soaked strands of hair off her face. "And no one stuffs apples down their chest like you do."

She tried hard not to laugh but failed. "I ought to kick you for that mean trick, you wretched man. I don't know how you did not fall to the ground hysterical, you must have been silently laughing so hard."

"Perhaps there was a little chuckle at your expense, but mostly the jest was on me. I watched you and never felt so at peace and happy as in that moment. I knew I was falling in love with you. I've done nothing but worry about how and when and *if* to ever tell you because I was afraid of one day breaking your heart. But I know now that it will never happen."

"How are you so sure?"

"Because my heart always knew you were the perfect one for me. It would not let me love anyone else. Nor would it ever allow me to marry anyone else. I had to wait for you."

"I'd always wondered about that. Marriage rumors were always swirling about you and some heiress or other, but nothing ever came to pass."

"You always got in the way."

"It's hard to believe. I am far from perfect. My behavior has been less than sterling. I ran off and almost drowned. I have every Bow Street runner in London searching for me. I've put you in danger and disrupted your life completely. If that isn't enough, I drank too much mulled wine and stuck my head in my supper dish. I've made an utter fool of myself."

He laughed. "Katie, are you serious? Was there ever a bigger fool born than I? And I would not consider marrying you if you were truly foolish. I cringe at the thought of the idiot children we would raise if that were so. If they turn out clever, it will be your doing. If they turn out beautiful, it will also be your doing. Same if they turn out warm, loving, and compassionate."

"What about your virtues?"

He rolled his eyes. "I have none, except that I have excellent taste in choosing my wife. I am wildly in love with you, and I don't see that changing anytime ever."

She threw her arms around him and hugged him fiercely. "Niall, I love you so much. I always have. Even when I did not like you."

"That is quite a recommendation." He wrapped his arms around her and drew her up against his body. The moment was not quite as romantic as he hoped it would be, for they were both soaking wet and Katie was now shivering.

Perhaps she was shivering a little from desire, but mostly she was cold. He had to get those clothes off her. But first this. "Kiss me, Katie."

She reached up on tiptoes and pressed her lips to his.

He took over from there, crushing his mouth to hers and allowing every ounce of love he felt for her to flow into their kiss. He plundered her lips, devoured the cherry sweetness of them, and claimed possession of her heart.

She had no choice but to surrender.

But she was not the only one conquered.

She had vanquished him long ago.

And now he was kissing his Perfect Miss Pringle.

In all his years of experience, there had never been a kiss more beautiful than hers. There had never been any as right and heartfelt as hers. But this was Katie. The kisses they shared would always be pure and innocent and joyful, given only to him, as his would only ever be given to her from this day forward.

He'd wanted to make their first kiss special and romantic, but they were both dripping water on the floor and their boots were squishing whenever they moved…another reason why he loved Katie. For someone as proper as she'd always been, she managed to get herself into the most improper situations. Mostly with him, of course. But she never seemed to mind being led astray when he was the one leading her.

She trusted him.

He would never betray her trust.

He deepened the kiss, drew her firmly up against him so that her wet shirt pasted to his chest. Water seeped into his clammy skin. It was the most uncomfortable kiss he'd ever given or received, and it was still the best.

Katie began to shiver from cold.

He ended the kiss and eased her out of his arms. "I'm going to help you out of your wet clothes now, Katie."

"You're going to undress me?" Her smile was as bright as a sunbeam.

He was trying to be serious and she looked like an excited child just given the best gift ever. "Do you mind?"

She shook her head and laughed. "Do I look like I mind? I've been dreaming of this moment for years. I never believed it would happen."

"Nor did I," he muttered. "Katie, that's all I'm going to do with you. I will get you out of your clothes and then wrap you in Mrs. Mablethorpe's robe. There will be no wicked night of sex for us until we exchange marriage vows."

She could not hide her surprise. "Why does it matter? I've accepted to marry you. You did offer, didn't you?"

"Yes. But your father hasn't accepted me yet. And let us not forget Yardsley."

"Oh, him. Kindly do not remind me of that oaf." Her smile faded.

"Niall, this may be the last night we have to spend together. Once we are on the road, we'll likely ride straight through to London. Will you not give me one night of pleasure in your arms?"

He glanced toward the bed. "I'll share it with you. But that is all. It's for your own protection." She would be put through enough shame once they arrived in town, he refused to make it worse for her.

Her family would likely require her to be examined by a physician to ascertain her state of innocence or lack thereof. To be put through this ordeal would be humiliating enough. He was not going to add to her burden by claiming her maidenhead tonight.

The scandal of being a runaway bride was bad enough. Yardsley would crush her if she returned unchaste.

Katie did not deserve to be treated this way.

He tugged the shirt out of her waistband and drew it over her head. Her bosom was still wrapped in the binding she'd used to hide her breasts, but this did not stop his heart from pounding a hole through his chest.

Katie's body was glorious.

His hands shook as he nudged her into a chair and bent to remove her boots and stockings.

He took a deep breath and moved away from her temptation to set the boots and stockings out to dry, then did the same with his, removing all of his garments except for his breeches.

He returned to Katie's side and knelt in front of her. She hadn't moved from her spot, sitting still as a statue, her hands in a death grip holding onto the sides of her chair and her eyes as wide as saucers.

Smiling, he leaned forward and kissed her on the lips.

She responded with aching sweetness, her mouth soft and giving as he pressed his lips to hers. He felt her love, felt it in the innocent warmth of her kiss.

Surely, he did not deserve her.

He slowly unfastened the binding that hid her lovely bosom, giving her the opportunity to change her mind. But she had no doubts, not even the flicker of hesitation as he peeled the fabric away to reveal the creamy fullness hidden beneath.

"Blessed saints," he said in a ragged whisper, trying to slow the fire raging through his already taut body.

He loved the softness of her skin and the silken length of her hair that now cascaded over her breasts because she was shy and was trying to hide her attributes. "Don't, sweetheart." He cupped the soft mounds in his hands and eased back to look at her.

She was so achingly beautiful…every inch of her.

When he drew his hands away, she immediately tried to cover herself again.

"Katie, let me look at you." Her breasts were round and firm and lovely in their fullness. Their tips were a soft, rose pink.

He moved closer and took one of those rosebud tips in his mouth, gently suckling it. She responded like a little volcano, almost leaping out of her seat, which she would have done had he not put his hands around her waist to steady her.

She clutched his hair and tugged on it, but she was tugging him toward her, not trying to push him away. "Niall!"

Still, this was new to her and he should have gone slower…shouldn't have touched her at all. But his resolve seemed to have washed away with the pounding rain. He drew his mouth away. "Do you want me to stop?"

"No…I…" She blushed. "Could you move on to the other breast?"

He laughed. "Yes, ma'am. Ever your dutiful servant."

He drew its already straining bud into his mouth, licking it lightly with his tongue before closing his mouth over it and teasing it between his lips. At the same time, he ran the rough pad of his thumb over the other creamy mound.

"Oh, my heaven," she said in a breathy whisper, now squirming in her seat. "I never knew what all the fuss was about. I never dreamed it would be like this."

He undressed her the rest of the way, his heart about to blow a hole in his chest as her glorious perfection was revealed.

Indeed, she was the Perfect Miss Pringle.

Hadn't he always said so?

"Katie, you're so beautiful," he whispered, closing his mouth over hers to kiss her long and hard. He had meant to be gentle, but she aroused such depths of feeling in him, he feared all his good intentions had been shot to hell.

She tasted of roast beef and mulled wine.

She felt like silk.

Her body was pink and cream except for the patch of dark curls at the junction of her thighs and the long, tumbling curls of her hair.

He carried her to bed and tucked her under the covers while he finished undressing and setting the rest of their clothes to dry. When he climbed in with her, he took her in his arms so that her body nestled against his. "Katie, we ought to sleep."

She laughed softly. "Not a chance, my wicked earl. I want to soak up every precious moment of my time with you. I almost drank myself into a stupor trying to work up the courage to seduce you...not that I would know how. I don't even recall what I said to you, probably something inept and embarrassing."

"You decided to give yourself to me without terms or restrictions."

"Sounds like something I would say."

"I refused. I want those terms and restrictions. I want to marry you and honor you for as many years together as we are granted."

"So do I. But I still love this, Niall. Being in your arms, baring my heart and body to you. I should feel wanton and ashamed, but I don't."

He turned on his side to face her, taking a moment to watch the play of firelight on her face. The warmth of the fire's glow reflected in her eyes. Truly, she looked like an angel. His angel. "I need to kiss you again, Katie."

"Yes, please do. And don't hesitate to take up where you left off before you finished undressing me."

He shouldn't. It would be a mistake to savor her body and arouse the passion that had lain dormant within her until tonight.

"I'm only going to kiss you," he said with utter conviction, hoping to force himself to hold to the resolution if he spoke it aloud.

It took him under five minutes to break it, for that was as long as it took for him to plant a sweet, safe kiss on her lips, then feather a trail of sweet, but less safe kisses along her neck, stop to lightly nibble the throbbing pulse by her throat, then kiss her breasts, and suckle and tease them to evoke her exquisitely torrid, soft gasps of pleasure.

He knew then that kissing her was no longer enough.

He wanted her to know a woman's pleasure.

Her body was already hot for him. She was on the edge of her first release and he wanted very badly to send her tumbling. So he touched her at her most intimate spot, knowing she had to be slick and ready for him. He used his fingers because – heaven help him – he dared not use his mouth.

He would turn into a mindless, devouring beast the moment he tasted her nectar.

Besides, he did not wish to tear his gaze away from her beautiful face. Or her eyes that shimmered with wonderment over her newest adventure. Being Katie, she held back nothing as he slowly stroked her sensitive nub.

She sighed and cooed, and revealed her heart.

He was fascinated by her delight, knew her moment was near as she gripped the sheet and held fast, moaning. She arched as the pressure built inside of her, and then she finally shattered into a thousand noisy points of starlight.

He kissed her on the mouth, partly because he wanted to kiss her anyway. He kissed her because he loved her as he'd never loved anyone or anything in his life.

But he also kissed her because he did not want anyone to hear her and start hunting for ghosts behind the walls.

She cast him an endearing smile as she began to calm. "I had no idea this is what I was missing."

He was not in the least calm, wanting to bury himself inside her, conquer her and claim her as she'd wholly claimed him. But he dared not, so he tucked his arms around her and drew her against his body, stifling a groan as her breasts pillowed against his chest. "There's more."

She nodded. "I know. It is obvious your needs have not been addressed."

"Nor will they be tonight," he growled and almost shot off the bed when she touched his arousal. "Katie, don't."

She quickly drew her hand away as though she'd touched it to a flame. "I'm sorry."

"You needn't be. It's just that…this is something that will have to wait for our exchange of vows."

"Why?"

"Because it is important to me."

"Very well." She smiled at him again. "Who ever thought you'd be the prude? But I'm glad you decided not to hold back on all of it."

He caressed her cheek. "I meant to. Shows you how weak my resolve is when it comes to you. Only with you, Katie. I want you to know this."

"I do know." She leaned over and softly kissed his chest over the spot of his heart. "I always knew you were wonderful. You just managed to hide it very well for a very long time."

He kissed her on the forehead. "Get some sleep. We both need it badly."

"Will you wake me in the morning with a kiss?"

"Yes, love. With a dozen of them…and other things that come to mind."

She was asleep within minutes, but he still had a fire raging through his loins – which he dared not address while Katie's soft body was pasted to his – so it took him longer to calm down and drift off.

He awoke a few hours later to an unaccustomed obstruction in his bed.

It took him a moment to realize he was in bed with Katie, his arms wrapped around her waist and he was using her body as a pillow.

Oh, lord! Had he crushed her?

Was she breathing?

He watched the gentle rise and fall of her chest.

Lord help him!

He wanted her with such agonizing ache.

He groaned softly and rolled back against his pillow. She scooted against him, her body seeking the warmth of his. He ought to have insisted she sleep in the borrowed robe, but Katie could be stubborn when she wanted to something badly enough.

And she wanted this night of nakedly sleeping in his arms.

Her wicked adventure.

He ran his hand lightly over her hair, frowning when he realized it was still damp. No wonder she was clamoring for his heat. He held her against him, trying to surround her in his warmth, and made certain to tuck the covers securely around her. "I love you, Katie," he muttered and fell back to sleep.

At dawn, he was awakened by Katie's shivers.

He turned worriedly and pressed a hand to her forehead.

She was burning up.

CHAPTER TWELVE

NIALL IMMEDIATELY TOSSED more logs onto the fire to heat the room and chase the dampness from it. He took a quick moment to open the shutter just a crack, enough to peer out the window. He knew it was morning, although the sky was too dark to tell the hour, for the rain was still coming down in buckets. The wind was so strong, it drove the rain at a slant across the window panes, pelting them with an unrelenting *pickety-pok.*

He turned back to Katie. "Love, I'm going to dress you."

"I'll do it," she said and tried to rise, but she was as weak as a newborn lamb.

He returned to her side. "Lie back. You have a fever."

She nodded. "My skin feels as though it is burning, but my insides are so cold."

Fortunately, her clothes had dried overnight and so had his. He dressed her in one of his shirts, then helped her to don her stockings, and wrapped her in the borrowed robe that was merely a sturdy linen and would not provide all that much warmth. He hoped it would be enough once he swaddled her in the blanket for added measure.

He then dipped some water from the ewer onto one of the wash cloths, wrung it out, and placed it over Katie's brow. He added his pillow to hers to prop her up because he did not want her sleeping flat. If this was a lung infection, she would need to sleep almost sitting up so the liquid did not collect in her lungs.

He settled her as best as he could and then dressed himself, intending to seek out Mrs. Mablethorpe. There was a risk he'd be seen, hopefully only by the loyal staff if he took the back stairs directly into the kitchen.

But first, he had to figure out a way to get through the door of the hidden room without knocking over the vase of flowers or the decorative, small table upon which the vase rested. Mrs. Mablethorpe would have put them back in place when she'd left them last night in order to hide the opening in the wall.

Just as he was puzzling it out, the door opened and the woman herself lumbered in with breakfast tray in hand. Niall took it from her. "Thank you. I was coming to find you. Katie has a fever."

"Oh, the poor lass. Well, there's tea here for her, some scones, honey, and marmalade jam. Oatmeal, too. That ought to hold her for now. I'll bring up some broth and soft bread later. An apple as well, but cut away the peel before ye give it to her."

"May I trouble you for another blanket and some more pillows?"

The kindly woman glanced at Katie who had fallen back asleep. "Yes, I'll fetch those right away. Anything else ye might need?"

"Some books and a deck of cards for me. The latest newspaper when it arrives." He lifted the lid over one of the plates to reveal a hearty portion of eggs and sausages. The other plate, obviously intended for Katie, held the same. However, Niall did not think she could handle it in her condition. She was safest eating the lighter fare of scones with jam. "Looks delicious, Mrs. Mablethorpe. I cannot thank you enough for your hospitality."

"We aim to please, m'lord. We'll do our best to get your young lady better again. The weather's so bad, I doubt my Douglas and his coach will arrive for another day or two yet. Then he'll have to wait for the roads to dry a bit before venturing out again. The delay will give her time to mend before you continue to London."

He nodded. "Indeed, she'll need all her strength for the battle to come once we're back in London. I'll do what I can, but I have not endeared myself to her father over the years."

"True love always finds a way, m'lord. That sweet girl will be fighting for ye as hard as ye will fight for her. It is refreshing to see a love match among the upper class. So many pass this way, husbands and wives who married for all sorts of reasons, nothing to do with love. Ye see the unhappiness in their eyes. Ye see the sadness in their children." She sighed and hurried off to fetch the pillows and blanket.

She returned soon with those items along with the cards and newspaper he'd requested. "That ought to hold ye for now, m'lord. I'll bring up some books with yer midday meal. Mr. Mablethorpe just told me that your horses returned. I hope it doesn't mean those wretched men will return as well."

"Hide the horses elsewhere. We'll figure out what to do if they come back here and persist in sticking around." He gave the woman a kiss on the cheek. "Truly, we are grateful for your kindness."

She blushed and hurried away.

When the wall slipped back in place, he strode to Katie's side and added the additional pillows beneath her and tucked the extra blanket around her slight, shivering body. The fire had taken hold and the room was too hot for him, but Katie needed the heat.

Fortunately, despite the rain, the air in the room was no longer damp.

He replaced the wet cloth on her brow with a fresh one, then settled himself at the table beside the shuttered window and ate his breakfast. Katie was sleeping comfortably and he saw no reason to disturb her when she did not appear to be in any distress. Most important, her chest appeared to be clear, no wheeze or shortness of breath.

He held out hope it was no more than a fever that would run its course in a matter of days. They were trapped here anyway for the next few days.

"Katie, how do you feel?" he asked when she began to stir. He went to her side and sat beside her on the bed to feel her forehead. The damp cloth had dried somewhat from the heat of her brow, but it had done the trick. Her fever had subsided quite a bit.

"Much better than a little while ago. I'm not shivering any more." She noticed the sweat beaded on his brow. "The room's too warm for you."

He nodded. "It doesn't matter. You're the one who needs to heal. Would you care for some tea and a bite to eat?"

She nodded.

He served her tea and a marmalade scone which she nibbled at and left most of it unfinished. But she drank most of the tea which he'd sweetened with honey. It was enough for now. A half hour later, she had some apple slices also dipped in honey.

"Niall, you are a man of many talents," she said, her smile quite affectionate. "I don't think I've ever been tended to as well as this. I marvel at this compassionate and caring side of you hidden all these years."

"No, I'm basically an arse." He caressed her cheek. "You manage to bring out the best in me."

She sat up and wrapped her arms around her knees, grinning impertinently. "And I am proud to say you bring out the worst in me. It feels good to finally be myself. Oh, I know I'm not really bad at all, but neither am I the buttoned up mouse everyone tried to make of me."

He kissed her on the nose. "You certainly were not that last night."

She blushed, obviously thinking of her discovery of passion. "No wonder women are so easily led to ruin. It was most enjoyable. I'm sorry

I've fallen sick."

"It isn't your fault. Anyway, I wasn't going to ruin you worse than I already did. I hadn't meant to go that far. Truly, Katie. You are something rare and precious. I was afraid to kiss you because I knew where it would lead."

"I'm glad you have no resolve and succumbed to my allure."

She was jesting, but he wanted to be serious for a moment. "You are alluring. You're the most beautiful woman I've ever beheld. Not just outwardly, but inside as well. This is why I want us married before I claim you. I don't know how else to show you how important you are to me and how much I admire and respect you. You deserve to experience our bonding as my wife, nothing less."

"Very well, since it seems quite important to you. But you are showing me your respect in everything you do for me. No man has ever cared for me the way you have. I'm no more than a bank account to Yardsley or any of the others who have courted me. Well, they've courted my bank account." She laughed softly. "It's ironic that my father sees you as a fortune hunter when you're the only one who ever bothered to know the real me."

"But it took me this long to come around. Rather pathetic, don't you think?"

She shook her head in denial. "You had your own growing up to do, finding out who you were. Your parents were not the best example of adult responsibility."

He winced. "That is true enough."

"But I am sure we shall be wonderful parents and our children will adore and worship us."

"Ah, Katie. They will love their mother for certain." He kissed her on the cheek, but drew away before he sought more. "Care to play cards? We're trapped here anyway until the rainstorm subsides."

"Do I dare play with you?" she asked when he grabbed the deck and began to shuffle it with the expertise of a cardsharp.

"Of course, I'll go easy on you since it is just for fun. We can play the less complicated games. Snip, Snap, Snorem? Or Battle? Or My Sow's Pigg'd? Bezique? Vingt-Un?" He continued to mix the deck, his hands working the cards like a magician so that he seemed able to pull out whatever card or suit he desired at will.

"I see how you spent your time in London at your clubs."

"It became a necessity as my father's health was failing and he seemed determined to destroy my inheritance with his reckless wagers. So I made it a point to win back as much as he had lost, or at least stem the tide of his losses."

Her gaze grew troubled. "I'm so sorry."

"Wasn't your fault." He shrugged. "Since you happen to be flat broke, I suggest we play for something other than money."

She tipped her head up in mock indignation. "I have plenty of money. I'm an heiress. I just don't happen to have any of it on me at the moment."

"We shall play for kisses," he said with a chuckle. "If I lose, I must kiss you."

"And if I lose?"

"You must kiss me."

A gleam of mirth sprang into her eyes. "I'm sure there is a flaw in your logic. I have a fever, so I do not think kissing on the lips is a very good idea."

He arched an eyebrow. "Then I shall kiss you elsewhere on your person. There are two prominent possibilities I have my eye on right now."

She smacked him playfully. "Do not stare at my chest!"

"Shows what a wicked mind you have. I was speaking of your hands."

She laughed softly. "Teach me how to play *Vingt-Un*. My brothers sometimes played it after supper. It did not look difficult. And being a tradesman's daughter, I ought to be able to figure out the odds easily enough."

They played for half an hour until Katie began to yawn and he put a halt to the game. "Get some rest, love. We'll resume later if you're feeling up to it."

Niall, having lost – Katie accused him of losing on purpose, which he had – gave her a chaste kiss on the cheek.

The rest of the day passed without incident, Katie sleeping for most of the time. She woke on occasion to eat or play another round of cards with him. He also read to her, but the drone of his voice always put her quickly back to sleep, so he read mostly to himself.

She hadn't asked about the latest newspaper accounts of her disappearance. There was nothing new. Same reward offered. Same speculation as to where she might have run off. Essex. Herfordshire. Kent. Surrey. Or perhaps she had never left the city of London. Few believed she had made it all the way up to Northumberland on her own.

But those two Bow Street runners had gotten on her trail fairly quickly. The young one, Standish, was no threat. He did not know how to think on his own, merely followed the more experienced man.

But Digby, the older one, was no fool.

Niall worried that Digby was going to double back to the inn and sniff about for sign of them. Mr. Mablethorpe was the weak link and he doubted it would take this experienced Bow Street runner much time to figure this out.

They were well hidden here and not about to come out anytime soon. Assuming no one accidentally tattled, they would work out a plan when the time came to sneak Katie into the carriage.

The Bow Street men knew what he looked like, but they hadn't set eyes on her. At best, they had a general description of her given by her parents. Perhaps they were shown a portrait, but it would have been done several years ago, before she had filled out in her womanly curves.

He also noticed an item of interest in the society pages. Yardsley had already taken up with some other heiress.

Good.

One less problem to deal with.

Yardsley and Katie's father must have formally severed the betrothal ties. If the unfaithful cur was free to pursue another 'mouse' then Katie was free as well. He set aside the newspaper and watched her as she slept.

Even when ill, she looked splendid.

He touched her forehead.

The fever was already subsiding. He hoped she would shake it given another day of rest. The broth and soft bread were the most she could manage, but she did finish them. To his relief, the fever did not spike upward at night.

She spent the night sleeping in his arms.

He told himself it was the best way for him to monitor her fever, but holding her through the night was a balm to his heart. He was completely lost to her. No, not lost. Belonged. It was the first time in his life he ever felt he belonged to someone. It was also the first time he felt responsible for someone.

He liked the feeling very much, even though it was a stark reminder of how empty his life had been before Katie had dramatically reappeared in it.

His parents were not terrible people and had loved him in their own way, to the extent they were capable of it. They did not beat him nor did he ever lack for material needs. But they were so caught up in their own misery, they could not see beyond themselves to properly care for anyone else. His father had lived a reckless life and his mother had spent her entire life in mourning for a husband who was never coming back to her.

Perhaps if she had been stronger, shown more spirit and chased him down to London, made him face up to his responsibilities as a husband and father. But it was too late now. They'd both passed on several years ago.

He would never, ever repeat his father's mistakes with Katie. Nor was Katie the mouse everyone had tried to shape her to be.

She was going to be formidable once she gained confidence in herself.

He couldn't wait to see her become the person she was meant to be.

By the next morning, the sun was shining and Katie's strength was returning. "What is that great yellow ball in the sky," she said, shading her eyes against the glare when he opened the shutter to peek out.

"Good morning, Miss Pringle. I trust you had a pleasant sleep."

She cast him a glowing smile. "A most excellent sleep. I had the most comfortable pillow. Who knew hard muscle made the best head rest?"

He walked over to the bed and kissed her brow. "And I had the prettiest, snoring lump at my side."

"Oh, no!" She covered her face with her hands. "Do I snore?"

"Delightfully."

She lowered her hands and sighed. "Does this mean we will have separate chambers once we marry?"

"Not a chance. I want you in my bed. I don't care if you snore like a foghorn. I don't care if you take all the covers or kick me in my sleep. I don't care if you curl up against me or push me off the bed. I want you there. Always."

She nodded. "I will be. I promise you."

He kissed her again.

She still had a light fever, but was much improved since yesterday. He would not be as worried now if they had to go back on the run. It would not happen today, for the ground was still flooded and too muddy for the carriages to manage. Another day would do it, then they would get back on the road to London.

"Niall, you are pacing like a caged tiger."

"I don't mean to be. I'm eager to be done with this chase and return to town. Your father isn't going to accept your marrying me. I'm just trying to figure out how to make it happen without having to take you on the run again."

He picked up the newspaper and turned to the society page where he'd seen the article about Yardsley. "But you won't have to worry about your betrothed. He's a man about town again. I think he and your father must have mutually agreed to rescind the marriage contract."

"Let's hope so. That would be one less hurdle to overcome."

He returned to peek out the shuttered window while she perused the paper. The inn was quiet today, few guests arriving or leaving because of the road conditions. But two obviously weary riders did stop at the inn. "Bollocks. Digby and Standish have returned."

"Mrs. Mablethorpe has hidden us well. We ought to be safe."

He raked a hand through his hair. "It's her husband I'm worried about. Digby is clever and knows how to get people to talk, as any good Bow Street runner would. Mr. Mablethorpe might let something slip. Let's hope his wife makes sure to keep them apart for the rest of the day. We should be out of here by tomorrow morning."

Katie eyed him with grim determination. "Unless we have to go on the run tonight."

"No, you still have a fever. I'm not dragging you out of here until our morning coach is ready."

"Hopefully, there will be no need. But I'm not going to let them catch us. I will allow no one but you to return me to my father."

"For the reward? Damn it, Katie. I don't want your father's money or Yardsley's. All I want is you."

She rolled her eyes. "Honestly, how did you ever earn the reputation as a fortune hunter? You are quite miserable at it."

CHAPTER THIRTEEN

ALTHOUGH KATIE WOULD have preferred a quiet ride back to London, she had to admit that dodging the Bow Street runners was quite a bit of fun. Niall had it all planned out, as she knew he would, for his brain was plotting their escape the entire time they ate their supper.

He'd left the room to explore the inn earlier in the day and knew Digby and Standish were still there, just waiting for one of them to show their face. "Digby's certain we are here. He keeps trying to talk to Mr. Mablethorpe, but his wife must have threatened him with death if he gives us away. He's closed up tighter than a clam shell."

"Poor man," she said with a laugh after hastily swallowing a spoonful of her broth. "Well, we will soon be gone from here and then he can chatter to his heart's content."

They were both seated at the small table beside the window, talking as they ate the meal brought in by Mrs. Mablethorpe.

Katie had felt well enough to climb out of bed, although her appetite had not fully returned. It would eventually. The fever had turned into more of a head cold, so even though she was hungry, she could not handle anything heartier than a broth.

Her eyes were watery, throat scratchy, and her nose was red from having to blow it constantly.

Her ears were stuffed, too.

And yet, Niall looked at her as though she was the most beautiful woman he had ever beheld in his entire life.

She'd never dreamed a man could feel this way about her.

Of all men, this wicked earl?

She could hardly believe it herself.

The London odds makers would be kept busy placing bets on them. Or rather, betting against them. How long before Alnwick is unfaithful to his wife?

One night?

One week?

One month?

It made her sad to think she was the only one who'd wager he never would be.

Niall was digging into his shepherd's pie with gusto. "The innkeeper's son arrived an hour ago with his coach," he said, talking between bites. "We'll be off tomorrow morning. But we won't leave at dawn. Digby will be expecting that and watching for us. We're going to wait until the inn gets busier, around ten o'clock in the morning."

She had been delicately sipping the broth, but set her spoon aside and paid closer attention to the planning. "Hoping to get lost amid the carriages pulling in with new guests and most of this evening's guests riding out?"

"Yes, partly." He drank some of his ale.

"But he'll recognize you, Niall. Then he'll know I must be nearby. He knows I was in disguise as Caleb. He'll be looking for any boy with his cap pulled down over his ears who climbs into the same coach as you."

"True, if he and Standish were here to see us."

She frowned. "Where would they be?"

"You forget the damage they did to the inn's property when they tried to catch us last time. Do you recall the door they broke down?"

She nodded. "The inn's finest guest room. I loved that room. But it is out of commission until that door is repaired. We offered to pay for it."

"Yes, and *I* shall. I brought you here. It is my responsibility to make it right." He cast her a warning glance when she opened her mouth to protest. "However, we did not break that door. Digby and Standish did. They ran off after us without paying for the damage."

"But Mr. Mablethorpe must have demanded it of them when they returned."

Niall shrugged. "I'm sure he did. I expect they reluctantly coughed up whatever they owed. But their actions were still criminal. Mrs. Mablethorpe has arranged for the magistrate to come by and haul them away tomorrow morning around ten o'clock."

Katie liked the plan.

It was remarkably simple.

He cast her a smug smile. "They'll be busy explaining their way out of their vandalism charge to the magistrate as we ride away. Magistrate Mablethorpe is going to hold them for a day or two before releasing them."

She burst out laughing. "You are diabolical."

"No, just well connected."

"How many more Mablethorpes are there in Thirsk? You seem acquainted with all of them. Indeed, the Mablethorpes treat you as though you are a long lost son. There is nothing they would not do for you. What is the reason?"

He drank a little more of his ale. "I happened to be here many years ago when their stable accidentally caught fire and their son, Douglas–"

"The one who is going to drive us to London?"

Niall nodded. "Yes. He was a boy at the time. I wasn't all that much older. Just starting university, but I was on my way to Alnwick during one of the term breaks. I had stopped here merely to rest my horse and grab something to eat before riding on. Meanwhile, a particularly skittish horse Douglas was tending to kicked over a lantern. The hay burst into flames and those flames quickly spread along the wooden beams. Within moments, the stable was on fire and Douglas was trapped inside. I ran in, got him and the horse out while the other stable hands got the rest of the horses free. They lost the stable, but nothing else."

She reached out and touched him lightly on the shoulder. "I wondered about that scar. No wonder they will do anything for you. Douglas would have perished if not for you. Why did you never tell us?"

He shrugged. "Should I have?"

"Yes, it was a very brave thing you did."

She saw his eyes fill with pain, but it lasted only a moment before his usual carefree manner returned. "I tried to tell my parents. They were too lost in their own concerns to care. When I arrived at Alnwick and boasted of it to my mother, she remarked that it was my father's fault this happened, because everything was his fault in her eyes. When I returned to London a few weeks later and mentioned it to my father, he asked if my horse had been injured. My *horse*. It never crossed his mind to ask about me even though I was still nursing my burns at the time."

Katie felt a tug to her heart. "I wish you had told me when I came up to Pringle Grange that summer. I would have repeated the story to everyone and remarked how brave you were. I was already infatuated with you, even though I wasn't certain I liked you. But this would have won me over. I would have even boasted about you to my kittens. I confided everything in them. They never gave away my secrets."

He chuckled, the flicker of pain now gone. "I'll make certain to come to you first next time I do something valiant. But we may both be old and gray before that happens again."

"I'm sure you do something brave and extraordinary every day."

He tweaked her chin. "I do not, although you bring out the best in me, as I've said before. Who knows? Anything is possible when I'm with you."

She toyed with her spoon, realizing they hadn't talked about the Swan and Maiden Inn. So she asked him about it now.

All warmth fled his handsome features. "It is an ugly business."

"I gathered as much."

He sighed. "They *befriend* young boys."

"Say no more." She clenched her fists. "I suspected as much, but could not imagine they would dare any such thing to a boy in the care of an earl."

"In truth, I did not either. But I'd had the bright idea to let on that you were mute and deaf, thinking myself very clever to make it a part of your disguise. They thought to approach you for this very reason. They did not believe you could tell me what they had done to you or even understand what they were doing and shout for help."

"Despicable fiends. I did not think I could ever shoot anyone, but those two would have proved me wrong. Is there anything that can be done about them?"

"I don't know, but I intend to look into the matter after I deliver you home to your family. Likely they are being protected by someone powerful in the area. What they do is common knowledge, yet no one has shut that inn down or imprisoned those men." He rose and stretched his strained muscles that were stiff from being in cramped quarters these past few days. "Let's deal with one problem at a time."

He leaned over and kissed her brow. "You safe first."

Later that evening, after the supper plates had been cleared away, she thought he would set up a pallet for himself on the floor. She was still constantly blowing her nose. But he settled in bed beside her and took her in his arms.

It felt wonderful, but also made her ache so badly.

They would be parted soon.

To be without him even for an hour seemed agonizing.

She nestled against his chest, fretting about what would happen once they reached London, but there was something quite soothing about being in his embrace and she quickly fell asleep to the steady rise and fall of his chest.

They awoke shortly after dawn to wash, dress, and pack their meager belongings in wait for their moment to escape. The opportunity suddenly came up, the magistrate arriving at the same time their coach drew up in front of the inn.

A moment later, Mr. Mablethorpe appeared and led them down the back stairs. "How are ye feeling, Miss Katie? Ye gave us all a good scare, falling sick as ye did."

She smiled at him. "I am much better, thank you. I'm sure it was your wife's excellent broth that did the trick."

She turned the collar up on her jacket and tamped the cap down over her eyes as she resorted to her Caleb disguise. Niall kept hold of her hand while they made their way to the inn's entrance hall that was now filled with departing guests.

They angled their way through the crowd and were almost at the coach when she heard one of the Bow Street runners shout, "There!"

Niall hoisted her into the coach and was about to climb in after her when the runners grabbed him. They gave him a shove to move him aside and reached inside to grab her. She punched Standish in the nose, but connecting her fist to his nose proved painful for her, too. "Ouch!"

She'd never thrown a punch before.

Someone ought to have warned her it bruised one's hand.

She was about to throw another punch when the fight suddenly stopped. It was over as quickly as it had started. Then she noticed the reason why. The magistrate had brought some of his men along to assist him with the arrest. They now had Digby and Standish subdued. "Add attempted abduction to the charges," she heard the magistrate intone. "And assaulting an earl."

Digby was desperately trying to explain who he was, but the magistrate refused to listen. "No! You don't understand! I'm a Bow Street runner! Don't let them get away!"

The magistrate did not appear at all moved. "My good man, I am not going to interrupt the Earl of Alnwick's travels without good reason. Unless he murdered your mother, I am going to send him off with my apologies for this disturbance."

Katie thought Digby would now expose her true identity, but he held silent and cast Standish a warning glance to hold his tongue as well.

Both Bow Street men were fuming as they were hauled away. "You fools! You–"

"Ah, another charge to add to your list of offenses," the magistrate said. "Insulting an officer of the law."

Digby paled. "But–"

"You can explain it in my office."

Niall was chuckling as he climbed in beside her. "You look confused, Katie."

The coach started rolling with a jounce as soon as Niall closed the door. She fell against his solid frame, but quickly sat up and stared at him. "I thought for sure Digby would tell him who I was."

He stretched his long legs before him and settled comfortably against the squabs. "Never. He's going to bargain to get out of there as soon as possible and ride to London as though the devil were on his tail. He'll try to catch up to us before we reach your father. He only needs to snatch you away at the last moment and be the one to deliver you to your dear papa. Then the enormous reward will be his."

"Poor man. He's earned it, don't you think?"

"I'm sure your father gave him a generous allowance to search for you. Your father and Yardsley should never have put up that damn reward. Men kill for far less. Who knows what Digby would have done if he'd caught you? Probably bound you up and stuffed you in a trunk to haul you back to London. I shudder to think what might have happened if others had caught on."

"Well, none of it happened and we'll be in London soon."

"I won't rest easy until the newspapers splash the news of your safe return across their banner headlines."

She stared at him.

He sighed. "I'm not taking the reward, Katie. Your tossing me the stink-eye will not change my mind."

"They are going to toss you out of the Fortune Hunter's Society."

He grinned. "I've been tossed out of worse places."

He put his legs up on the opposite seat, leaned his shoulder against side wall, and closed his eyes. She supposed this was his not so subtle hint he was not going to talk about the subject any longer. Since he was obviously hoping to sleep, she simply stared out the window to watch the passing landscape.

They did not stop except to change teams of horses and grab a quick bite. Niall and Douglas took turns driving the coach, each of them sleeping in shifts, so there was no stopping overnight at any inns along the way. Fortunately, the skies remained clear and the moon was still in its full phase, casting its silver light upon the ground.

The further south they rode, the more congested the roads became. But this also worked to their advantage, for these important main roads were lit by torches to mark the way for those traveling by night.

They arrived in London in the wee hours of the morning, their coach the only one clattering along the Thames embankment at this late hour.

Katie's heart skipped beats, her tension increasing when they finally turned onto her street in fashionable Mayfair. The Pringles were considered upstarts and had not been welcomed to the elegant square of homes that were all quite imposing and grand.

Her father, thumbing his nose at the *ton* elite, had purchased the largest and grandest of them all.

Niall helped her down from the coach when it drew up in front of the impressive townhouse. He kept hold of her hand as he walked her to the door and rang the night bell. She noticed the pistol he'd discretely withdrawn from his boot and now held in his other hand.

They'd made incredibly fast time from Thirsk to London. Digby and Standish could not have caught up to them. But others might have thought of watching the house and abducting her before she had the chance to enter. Really, that's all some enterprising scoundrel needed to do, grab her at the last moment and claim the reward.

She breathed a sigh of relief when a light appeared in the entry hall and in the next moment, their head butler opened the door. "Weston, let Father know I'm home," she said, removing her cap so he could see her face. "We'll wait for him in his study."

The dear man almost fainted. "Oh, Miss Katie! We were all so worried! Heaven be praised, you're safe!"

He stepped aside to allow them both in, then shut the door, handed them a lit candle, and hurried off to wake her parents.

Niall set the candle down on her father's desk and took her in his arms as soon as they entered the study. He gave her a fierce hug. "I may not have the chance to hold you like this again, at least not for a while. I love you, Katie."

She returned his embrace with equal ferocity. "I won't let anyone keep us apart."

"Nor will I. But give your father a little time to calm down before you make demands on him. He won't be thinking clearly just yet. He'll refuse anything you ask of him, especially if it has anything to do with me."

They said no more to each other while waiting for her parents.

They heard her father emit a roar followed by a thump of footsteps on the stairs. Her mother's softer cries could also be heard as she ran down behind her father. "Katie! Katie" they were both shouting as they hurried into the study.

She rushed to her parents and hugged them. "I'm so sorry I frightened you, but I couldn't marry Yardsley. I couldn't go through with the ceremony. I had to run."

"Don't ever put us through this again," her father growled as he hugged her and began to weep.

Her mother was already weeping.

Katie soon found herself in tears, too.

After a moment, her father noticed Niall. He'd been standing aside quietly while they reunited. "Alnwick! You? I might have known. What was your involvement in my daughter's sudden disappearance?"

Katie gasped. "Nothing! He saved my life and brought me safely back home, at great risk and inconvenience to himself, I might add."

Her father cast her a dubious look. "We'll see about that."

She frowned at him. "There is no question of his sacrifice on my behalf. He's earned the reward. Don't you dare renege on offering it to him."

"Now, Katie," they both said at the same time, then scowled at each other.

Typical stubborn men.

"This is not the time to speak of it," Niall said. "I'll come by in the morning at ten o'clock and we'll talk further. Does that suit you, Mr. Pringle?"

"Yes, it suits him," Katie answered before her father could refuse.

"Good, then I'll be off."

"Where will you go?" She realized he must be exhausted, for he and Douglas had only grabbed snatches of sleep over the last few days. "How thoughtless of me. We'll have rooms made up for you and Douglas right now. I'll–"

Niall held up a hand. "No, Katie. It isn't necessary. Douglas and I will return to my club. I keep a room there for when I'm in town."

Her father snorted in disdain.

She clenched her fists to stem her outrage. "Don't you dare–"

Niall cut her off again. "Katie, it's all right. We'll talk tomorrow. Get a good night's rest. I'll see you in the morning."

He nodded to her parents and strode out.

She heard the front door close behind him and it felt as though her own heart had closed down. "I love him," she murmured, knowing it was not the wisest comment to make just now. But she was not going to hide her feelings.

Her father turned apoplectic. "Katie Pringle, you don't know what you are talking about. That young man is a no-good, fortune hunting wastrel."

Her mother took her arm to lead her up to bed. "Katie, listen to your father. You've always been enamored of him, but you cannot trust him.

He's a Jameson. Oh, dear! Has he…taken liberties?"

Her father emitted an agonized cry. "Sweet mercy! What has he done to you, child?"

"Other than behave like a complete gentleman? He's done nothing untoward." Well, she certainly was not going to mention her first sexual experience which was no one's business but her own and Niall's. "If by liberties you mean has he taken my innocence? No, he has not."

Her parents exchanged looks.

At her mother's nod, her father said, "I'll have Dr. Farthingale come over first thing in the morning."

"Don't you trust me?" Tears welled in Katie's eyes.

"Of course, we do," her mother said, giving her an affectionate squeeze. "It's Alnwick we don't trust."

Katie's heart lurched in misery. Niall had known this would happen. This is why he had refused to engage in further intimacy. He did not want to see her put through this very shame. "I'm not the one you should be examining. Yardsley is the cheater, not me. He's the one who was unfaithful. Why do you think I ran off? I caught him…doing *that* with Sybil."

She studied their faces. "Oh, I see Yardsley did not bother to tell you. Nor would Sybil ever confess her role in humiliating me. I caught them together in the clerestory moments before our wedding was to take place. He did not have enough respect for me to wait even one day before making a mockery of our wedding vows. Not that I care anymore. I will never marry him. But there is one thing I would like to know before I retire to bed."

"And what is that?" her mother asked.

"Did he end our betrothal contract?"

CHAPTER FOURTEEN

NIALL STRODE OUT of the Wicked Earls' Club the following morning and climbed into the waiting coach Douglas Mablethorpe had brought around to the front. "You don't need to remain in London for my sake, Douglas. I know you have plenty of work to keep you occupied back home. I can easily have the club steward hail a hack for me."

He grinned and shook his head. "My mother will box my ears if I dare leave you now. I am at your service, my lord. Even if it means taking you and Miss Pringle north to Gretna Green."

"Hopefully, that will not be necessary." But it could not be ruled out, especially if Katie's betrothal contract had not be terminated.

He climbed in, giving thought to what he would say to Katie's father. He was also curious to find out what she had told her parents, if anything yet.

There was another carriage in front of the Pringle townhouse when they drew up. He knew it was not Yardsley's for there was no crest on the carriage door, and Yardsley never went anywhere without evidence of his rank and overly inflated importance.

He was admitted in by the head butler and immediately shown into the study to await Katie and her parents. It wasn't long before he heard voices in the entry hall and noticed someone leaving.

The sound of Katie's voice, pained and tearful, had him walking out of the study to see what was going on. She ran into his arms the moment she spotted him. "Katie, what's happened?"

"They brought a doctor to…"

She did not need to say anything more. He'd recognized the man who was walking out. Dr. George Farthingale. Had it been anyone else, he would have ripped the man apart. But he knew the doctor and had tremendous respect for him. He also knew Katie would have been treated as gently as possible by him, without judgement or condescension. "Dr. Farthingale."

"Good morning, Lord Jameson," the man said, eyeing him with remorse. "I'm truly sorry for putting Miss Pringle through…well, there's no doubt she was telling her parents the truth. Take care of her."

"I will." He held Katie as he watched the doctor stride out and climb into his carriage.

Still, that her parents had insisted on this examination left him feeling sickened. Katie, the sweet innocent, had been forced to endure this humiliation and it had overset her.

He frowned at them. "Time for us to talk seriously."

He led Katie into the study and waited for her parents to follow. She sank onto the settee and her mother did the same, settling beside her. Her father took his chair behind the large desk that dominated the room, as though this would give him greater authority.

Of course, Niall had never had much respect for authority and was never one to be intimidated anyway.

Besides, he was the earl and therefore the one in charge. He remained standing and immediately took control of the conversation. "You now know your daughter is innocent. Shame on both of you for ever doubting her. Has she told you why she ran off?"

"I did," Katie said, scowling at both her parents. "And I also related most of our adventures, starting with my falling in the river. But you'll be relieved to know that Yardsley has decided I am unworthy to be his marchioness and terminated our betrothal in my absence."

"Typical of that arse." Niall grinned. "I'll have to thank him for his lack of judgement. One less problem for us to deal with."

"Yes, the biggest one we would have had to face," she agreed. "There is no impediment to our marrying now."

Her father shot out of his chair. "Katie, let me handle this. There will be no marriage to this bounder, I assure you."

She leaped out of her seat. "Bounder? How can you call him that after all I've told you? He is the only man I trust and the only one I will marry. So put any other plans out of your head at once. I will have no other."

Her father's look was one of despair more than anger. "My child, think about what you are saying. He's a Jameson and will break your heart."

Her hands curled into fists as she stared down her father. "He will never break my heart. He will love me always because he is *Niall* Jameson and not his father or his grandfather. There is nothing you can say that will alter my opinion."

Niall's expression hardened. "Let me assure you, I will marry your daughter. For Katie's sake, I would appreciate your consent, but I will not be stopped by your refusal to give it."

"Is that so? We'll see how long it takes for you to change your tune when I cut her off completely. If you want Katie, then she is all you shall ever have. You will never receive so much as a ha'penny from me. What do you say to that?"

"I accept your terms."

Her father shook his head. "What?"

"Your terms are accepted. I will take Katie. I love her more than anything in this world. You can keep your money, every last ha'penny. I'll obtain the special license today."

Katie was incensed, as he knew she would be when he declined everything but her. She looked beautiful in her indignation, but what he loved most was the faith she had in him. A deep, unshakable faith that no one else had ever had in him. "You earned the reward! And what about my dowry? You cannot cut me off, Papa. My dowry is promised to me."

Niall did not want to engage in this conversation. He wanted to be off to obtain the license and haul a minister back here to conduct the ceremony this very day. "I am refusing the reward, Katie. I told you I would. As for your dowry, I have no intention of ever touching it so do not bother to fight over it. Your father can do with it as he pleases, put it in your name or hold it in trust for you. Or not give it to you at all. I don't care. I will provide for you."

"But–"

"No, I can manage without all of it. What I cannot manage without is you."

She cast him the softest smile and sighed.

"Are we agreed?" Niall did not want her to pursue the matter of the reward. First of all, Yardsley was unlikely to pay up his share without being chased to court. Frankly, he did not want the bastard's money. He did not ever wish to look upon any improvement to Alnwick and know it was accomplished because of Yardsley's filthy lucre.

As for her father, the man would spend the rest of his life convinced Niall had married his daughter for her fortune unless he declined all of it. No matter how many times she said he must have it, he knew he would have to refuse.

It was important for Katie's sake. He wanted her family to know he'd married her for love and not to ease his bank account. "You are the most precious thing in the world to me."

She rolled her eyes at him. "You are quite irritating."

He grinned affectionately. "Haven't I always been?"

She laughed despite wanting to remain irate. "Yes."

"And you've always been perfect," he said with a husky catch to his voice, his manner once again serious. He took her hands in his. "Will you have me, Katie? Life with me will be a struggle, but I can think of nothing better than to rebuild Alnwick with you by my side as my countess."

"And I wish to be nowhere else but at your side." Tears sprang into her eyes. "Yes, I will have you. I will love you and cherish you for all the days of my life."

"As I will always love and cherish you." He kissed her lightly on the lips. "Mr. Pringle, will you come with me to obtain the special license? And before you pass comment, I will pay for the license." He already considered Katie as bound to him just as he was bound to her. The ceremony would only proclaim to society what they already felt in their hearts and to the depths of their souls.

Her father stared at Katie for the longest time.

Her mother finally spoke up. "It is no use, my dear. Our Katie has her mind set on her Earl of Alnwick and there is no talking her out of it. She loves him. She has always loved him. I was wondering when she would finally realize it."

"But he's a Jameson," her father said weakly, knowing he was fighting a losing battle now that his wife had taken sides with his daughter.

"One who has always loved her, although it certainly took him long enough to figure it out," she said, casting Niall a shame-on-you look. "Almost too long. In truth, I was afraid your father had tainted your outlook on marriage to the point you could no longer recognize love when it slapped you in the face."

Niall nodded. "I won't deny he was a terrible influence on me."

Mrs. Pringle nodded. "All those years passed, all those summers, and you never said a word. My poor Katie gave up on you, deciding to move on and marry Yardsley. I thought she could be happy as his marchioness even though it was not a love match. I was wrong. Her heart is too soft. Only love will do for her. So, you have my blessing, for what it's worth."

"But he's a Jameson," her father repeated, albeit with less conviction.

Katie came to her father's side and gave him a hug. "Isn't it marvelous? Now you shall have your revenge on his father and grandfather for the shameful way they treated you. Think of it, Papa. What better revenge can you exact on them than to have your daughter marry into their family? I shall be the Countess of Alnwick."

"I never thought of it that way." His eyes lit up at the revelation. "You really want this, Katie?" He gripped her shoulders and regarded her solemnly.

She nodded. "With all my heart."

"Well then…" Her father gave a harrumph. "You never could hide your feelings. You are glowing like an incandescent little lamp."

"How can I not? He's wonderful and we love each other. And I know you are about to give in because you don't want me to be an unhappy spinster living alone in a big house filled with cats, walking around in a frayed lace gown covered in cat hairs and cloying perfume, thinking of nothing but faded memories."

"Katie, you are being ridiculous." Her father tried not to smile, for he was not yet ready to acquiesce to their union. But his lips twitched upward at the corners and it was only a matter of moments before he gave in.

"Say yes, Papa."

He groaned.

And hemmed and hawed.

Finally, he gave in.

"She's your problem now," he muttered, turning to Niall and holding out his hand. "Seems I've been outvoted on this matter. Welcome to the family, Alnwick."

Niall laughed as he shook his hand. "And I shall return the favor, Mr. Pringle. Welcome to my family. How does it feel to be related to a Jameson?"

"Pretty damn good, if you must know." He clapped Niall on the shoulder. "Come along, son. We have a special license to obtain."

Niall turned to Katie and winked. "Ready for your next adventure, my love?"

CHAPTER FIFTEEN

"DO YOU, NIALL Jameson, Earl of Alnwick, Viscount Darnelly, Knight of the Garter…" Niall never thought his wedding vows would be anything more than words to spout in order to get through the marriage ritual. They were words to be said without conviction because he never thought he would be marrying for love.

Nor did he believe for a moment that he was deserving of this good fortune. But Katie had been good all her life and apparently her wishes were being answered. He marveled that she would wish for him, but he silently vowed to never make her regret it.

He loved her so much, the feeling sang through his bones.

"You're a Knight of the Garter?" Katie whispered, interrupting the minister's recital of his titles, both hereditary and ceremonial.

He nodded. "Incredible, isn't it? Makes you wonder what our country is coming to."

She smothered a chuckle.

The minister scowled at both of them to quiet their chatter so he could continue. "Do you take Miss Katharine Pringle…"

"Yes, with all my heart," he said with enthusiasm, eager to embark on their new life together.

They were exchanging wedding vows in a quiet ceremony in her family's London townhouse. He held her hands all the while, promised to love, honor, and protect her, and silently resolved to let her know how much he loved her every day of their lives.

"Where are you taking my daughter?" Katie's father asked after the wedding breakfast was over.

Niall expected that he and Mr. Pringle would eventually be on excellent terms, but they were not there yet. He could not, absolutely would not, let the man know where he and Katie were going to spend their wedding night. "I'm taking her somewhere she's always wished to go."

Katie gasped and her eyes lit up. "Do you mean it?"

He grinned. "Yes, love. I mean it. The arrangements have been made."

Her father assumed they were going to one of London's finest hotel establishments and he allowed the man to continue to think so. To know the truth would have sent his heart into spasms requiring medical attention anyway.

Besides, whose business was it but his and Katie's what they did next?

Douglas Mablethorpe, whose discretion could be relied upon, took them in his coach to Bedford Place and the Wicked Earls' Club.

Niall would not have chosen this for himself, but he was indulging Katie's request. She had asked him to sneak her up to his private chamber at the club and he was not about to deny her what she considered an exciting adventure.

In the morning, he would relinquish his membership.

But tonight was Katie's to do with him as she wished. Besides, he was not going to complain if their surroundings emboldened her to be more adventurous in bed. With him only, of course.

He tried not to grin as they crept upstairs and down the hall to his chamber, for she was wide-eyed and thought she was being terribly naughty when she was not at all. He led her into the simple, but elegantly appointed room, and immediately shut the door. She took in her surroundings, practically inhaled them with her big eyes and soft, puckered mouth. "Is this where you carried on your depraved and debauched existence?"

He coughed. "Yes, Katie. But that was before I realized I loved you."

"You are forgiven."

He hadn't asked for forgiveness, but he accepted it graciously. "What do you wish to do now? This Wicked Earl is entirely at your service."

The fire was lit in the hearth. Champagne and a light repast had been set out for them. Fresh bedding. Fresh water in the ewer on his bureau. Other items had been left for them atop the bureau, but he quietly tucked those in a drawer. He hadn't asked for them, knowing they were a little too adventurous for his Katie. Besides, he did not need anything other than this beautiful girl in his arms to give him a night of unforgettable splendor.

The two of them were already ablaze with desire.

However, he was not going to rush her. They had all night for seduction and he meant to take his time and savor every moment.

Smiling, she walked around the room, sat on the bed to test it out. Bounced on the bed and laughed softly, the returned to his side and into his open arms. "Will you kiss me, Niall?"

Gad, this was her idea of a wild adventure? To sneak in and be kissed by her husband in his club. "Yes, love."

She gazed at him in raptures. "This will be a wonderful story to tell our grandchildren."

"Katie, are you mad? We mustn't breathe a word of this to any of our offspring, no matter how far down the generational ladder."

"Oh, but we must. *Chicks, did I tell you of the time your dashing grandfather kissed me in his Wicked Earls' Club?*"

"Just a kiss?" He arched an eyebrow. "Is this all you wish me to do?"

"Heavens, no. But to tell our grandchildren more would utterly corrupt them." She blushed. "Besides, I'm not sure what to do next. I think you ought to take over after our kiss."

"My pleasure." He brought his lips down on hers, meaning to be gentle as he tasted the honey-sweet promise of her kiss. But she overwhelmed him. What was meant to be gentle turned into something hot and crushing.

Lord help him! She turned him so fiery, they would be nothing but cinders by morning.

He struggled to temper himself, not wanting it all to be over in one quick, explosive burst. But he ached with need and she must have felt it as he ground his mouth against hers and felt the soft give of her own.

This was his Katie, soft and loving. Opening her heart to him. Trusting him and responding to his kisses with wholehearted enthusiasm.

He loved her faith in him.

It swelled him with pride and also humbled him that this treasure of a girl also valued him.

He ran his tongue lightly along her lips to tease them apart and then dipped his tongue into her mouth to mingle with hers in a slow dance he knew would soon build to a crescendo.

But first, he wanted to give her the chance to explore, to feel each mounting sensation, and understand the secrets held within their bodies. Secrets to be revealed as they surrendered to passion.

They had all night to enjoy each other, to engage in these mating dances that would bind their hearts and souls.

Their kisses grew hotter.

He began to undress her, undoing the laces and buttons designed to thwart any man lusting for her beautiful body. But he'd become fairly adept at this, not a talent he was particularly proud of except that it was useful at this moment.

The gown slipped off her shoulders, gliding down her body with a light *whoosh*. He lifted her up to untangle the pool of silk at her feet and set it aside. She was now left only in her undergarments.

Blessed saints!

She was so beautiful.

He stared at her perfect body outlined beneath the sheer fabric of her chemise, his gaze fixed upon the dusky tips of her breasts barely hidden and already straining for his touch. He cupped one of those creamy mounds and ran his thumb lightly over the tip, the rough pad of his thumb against the fabric adding to the friction.

She closed her eyes and moaned, her every feeling evident on her expressive face.

He set about removing her remaining garments one by one, softly touching, slowly trailing possessive kisses down her body, for she was now his, bound in heart and in law.

Yet, he was also completely hers. She possessed him. Heart and soul. If there was something beyond, she possessed that, too.

"I love you, Katie." He ran his hands along her silken skin, and repeated the words as he took the pins from her hair, watching the length of curls flow down her back unbound.

He buried his hands in those waves of dark silk and kissed her long and hard.

She responded immediately, her body now flushed and showing all the signs of arousal. He slipped the chemise off her, having left it for last for the sake of her modesty. His beautiful Katie wanted to be wicked and wanton, but she wasn't really. She had an ingrained bashfulness that he found most endearing.

It meant so much more that she was willing to shed her inhibitions for him alone.

He put his lips to her heart, feeling its rapid beat and then suckled her breast lightly before easing away. "Undress me, Katie," he said in a husky murmur.

She was already grasping at his jacket to tug it off him.

He helped her with the rest of it, allowing her to strip him naked and encouraging her to explore him and kiss him as he was doing with her. "Touch me as you would like me to touch you."

Her eyes widened in surprise, then she cast him a beautiful smile and ran her tongue lightly over his nipple.

Blessed saints.

Fire coursed through his body. He lifted her in his arms and carried her to bed, not bothering to draw aside the covers or settle her properly between the sheets before he settled atop her and began their mating dance in earnest.

She reached hungrily for him.

He meant to keep his resolve, to give her time to get used to him, to have her touch him and absorb the sensations, but they were too wild and desperate for each other. Next time they would take it slow and gentle.

Not this time.

Fiery bursts of pleasure were already rocking through his body.

She licked his nipple again.

"Bollocks, Katie." He gave a groaning laugh and settled between her legs, positioning her for his entrance. "You'd better not...not yet."

Her sparkling eyes stared back at him in confusion. "I thought you wanted me to."

"I do, love. But you're too tempting and I find I cannot wait." She was ready for him, he felt her slickness as he slid his hand down, thinking to prepare her.

Lord help him!

Her slick heat was arousing beyond measure.

She was simply beautiful, her eyes shimmering with love for him and her arms open and inviting.

He thrust in slowly, knowing she would feel some unease when he broke through her barrier. But Katie was never one to complain, nor did she now when after a few careful thrusts he broke through. "Katie, have I hurt you?"

"No. You never could." She caressed his cheek and whispered that she loved him.

The two of them now became one, lost in each other, lost to the night and all its splendor. Lost in the fiery explosions that came with their release. Two hearts given in love, two promises given that would never be broken.

She was his now, forever his.

He held her tightly, wrapped her hot body in his arms as he spilled his seed inside of her and told her how much he loved her.

Her long, dark hair spilled over the pillows.

Her smile lit up his heart.

Her eyes reflected the silver moonlight.

She looked like a sylph, a faerie maiden out of a dream.

They were both laughing as they slowly calmed in the aftermath. He caressed her body, her soft skin and slender limbs that entwined with his like a graceful vine around an oak. He kissed her lightly on the lips as he pulled out and eased his weight off her. "How do you feel, Katie?"

She nestled atop him, resting her soft breasts against his chest and grinned at him. "Your Perfect Miss Pringle has shattered into a thousand bursts of starlight. I feel happy. Euphoric. Ready for more adventures."

He gave a laughing groan. "Already?"

She nodded, then began to nibble her lip fretfully. "Unless this is all you can do tonight. You do look spent. Quite wrung dry."

He burst out laughing. "Spent? Dried out?"

She nodded again in earnest, apparently unaware that mating could occur more than once in a night.

He rolled her back under him and stroked her silky thigh. "I am ever at your service. I am *always* at your service. Close your eyes, my love."

He kissed his way down her body and proceeded to live up to his reputation as a Wicked Earl. He would gladly shed this mantle for that of faithful husband.

But for tonight, he was still a Wicked Earl, wicked only with his wife.

EPILOGUE

Alnwick Hall
Northumberland, England
October, 1821

NIALL STEPPED DOWN from Douglas Mablethorpe's coach as it rolled to a stop in front of Alnwick Hall. He helped Katie descend and they walked hand in hand toward the house. But they managed no more than a few steps before Mr. Crisp and his wife came running out to greet them. "Miss Katie!" Mrs. Crisp cried and clasped her to her ample bosom. "Is it really you? Saints be praised! He's brought you back to us."

Niall laughed. "She's Lady Katie now and she's here for good. We were married a fortnight ago in London."

"Married? Saints be praised!" she cried again and gave Katie another hug.

Mr. Crisp's eyes began to fill with tears. "It's a miracle."

In a more formal household, such familiarity would be deemed highly improper, but it could never be so at Alnwick Hall. For one, Katie would never allow it. She had the warmest heart, always filled with compassion for others.

Niall watched as the couple continued to fuss over her. "Do I not get a greeting or is my wife already your favorite and I'm to be tossed out into the cold?"

"She's a lamb and you are a wicked devil." Mrs. Crisp gave him an affectionate cuff on the shoulder before reaching out to give him a hug. "But you did very well for yourself, m'lord. There isn't a finer wife to be had. She's perfect for you. That's what I told Mr. Crisp the moment I saw the two of you together as children. Didn't I say so?"

Her husband nodded.

Katie grinned at Niall. "Seems everyone knew it except us."

He lifted her in his arms. "Fortunately, we figured it out eventually."

"Yes, I got the earl of my dreams."

"And I got the heiress of my dreams." He started to carry her toward the house.

She placed her arms around his neck. "I don't think you can make that claim when you are still refusing the reward. And now that my father has decided not to disown me, you still won't take my dowry."

"I've told him to put whatever he wishes in an account for you and our children. As for Yardsley's portion–"

"I can't believe he paid up. Perhaps he's had second thoughts about his behavior and is ready to reform."

Niall snorted. "Not a chance. But I have powerful friends who shamed him into paying it over. It's for you and your father to do with as you wish. I hope you'll give some to those who helped us on the way to London."

"Of course."

"Donate the rest as you wish. You're all I want, Katie. And I never want you to doubt it."

"You really are a discredit to fortune hunting scoundrels all over the world."

"You are wrong, love. I've found my fortune and intend to hold on to her with all my soul and strength. I knew as I carried you over the threshold the first time, you were the one for me. It felt very right, even though you were a wet, little lump and looked exhausted. But you also looked beautiful and I was beguiled."

She'd run here in her saddest moment. Niall understood now that she'd been running to him. Their hearts had always belonged together. He'd been too caught up in the Jameson misery to recognize this gift he'd almost lost.

He paused after crossing the threshold and gave her a kiss on the lips. "Welcome home, Countess Alnwick."

He was surprised to find her eyes tearing, for she'd been through so much and had not once complained or faltered. But he understood the enormity of her feelings and kissed her again.

She smiled at him, her beautifully captivating smile that never failed to leave him breathless. "Thank you, my lord. It's good to finally be home."

THE END

Dear Reader,

I hope you enjoyed Niall and Katie! Niall was a bit of a fortune hunting rogue, appearing as such in a few of my Book of Love series stories, The Touch of Love and The Kiss of Love. But I always knew Katie would be the one to bring out the good in him and redeem him. Niall is not my only Wicked Earl. I have two other Wicked Earls in this popular series, Earl of Westcliff and Earl of Kinross. Tynan Brayden is the Earl of Westcliff and his cousin, Marcus Brayden, is the Earl of Kinross. You will love these big, brawny Brayden men, and will find more of them as the heroes in my Book of Love series: Romulus in The Song of Love, Finn in The Scent of Love, Joshua in The Chance of Love, and Ronan in The Gift of Love.

Take a peek at the other books I have available and fall in love with your next Regency hero. Keep reading for a sneak peek at Lauren Smith's wonderful contribution to the Wicked Earls' Club series, The Earl of Morrey.

ABOUT THE AUTHOR

Meara Platt is a USA Today bestselling author and an award winning, Amazon UK All-star. Her favorite place in all the world is England's Lake District, which may not come as a surprise since many of her stories are set in that idyllic landscape, including her award winning, fantasy romance Dark Gardens series. If you'd like to learn more about the ancient Fae prophecy that is about to unfold in the Dark Gardens series, as well as Meara's lighthearted, international bestselling Regency romances in the Farthingale series and Book of Love series, or her more emotional Braydens series, please visit Meara's website at www.mearaplatt.com.

Sneak Peek at Lauren Smith's
Earl of Morrey
The Earl of Morrey
Chapter 1

Excerpt from the *Quizzing Glass Gazette*, September 10, 1822, the Lady Society column:

My darling ladies,

I have returned to bring you the most delicious gossip. It must be noted that the existence of a certain club has recently reached my attention, one called the Wicked Earls' Club. Only the most wicked of titled earls are said to be members. Naturally, my mind has run away with thoughts of a most dangerous nature. Who belongs to this club, and do you already know them? Is the polite earl you danced with last night at Lady Allerton's ball all that he seems? Is there more to the tall, dark-haired gentleman who tipped his hat as he rode past you in Hyde Park this fall?

I AM MIST. I am moonlight. I am the smoke of an extinguished candle. I am the shadow you do not see, but only feel . . .

Adam Beaumont, the Earl of Morrey, let the words of his private mantra flow over and through him until he believed them to be true. As he moved through the crowded ballroom of Lady Allerton's home, the words worked a subtle magic. They rendered him nearly invisible to the husband-hunting ladies prowling around him, their matchmaking mamas leading the hunt. Given that he was an unmarried, young, and attractive gentleman with a title, that was quite a feat. If the *ton* knew what sort of man he truly was, those young women and their mothers would not be so eager to snare him.

He swept his gaze over every face in the packed ballroom, seeking that cunning gleam in a pair of eyes or an overly observant glance in his direction. He listened carefully for clever discussions designed to collect information best kept hidden.

A loaded pistol would have been a welcome companion tonight, but he could not conceal such a cumbersome weapon on his person. No, the only friend he carried tonight was the slender dagger pressed flat against his chest beneath his waistcoat. He dared not risk a dance, lest the blade dislodge and become a danger to him.

If only the *ton* knew what sort of man stood in their midst. A man whose job was to end any threat to the Crown. An agent of His Majesty who worked to keep the monarchy safe, as well as to protect the kingdom from foreign threats. He was the knife in the dark that claimed the life of anyone who came here to do his nation harm. It was a burden Adam had never wanted, but he had been given little choice.

Many thought that wars started and ended on the battlefield, but Adam knew the darker truth. Wars began in drawing rooms and ballrooms, where men let down their guard and become targets for spies and assassins. He'd learned that after losing his friend Lord Wilhelm. It had been two years since he'd watched a French spy take the life of his dear friend.

John Wilhelm had struggled with a French assassin on a bridge over the Thames. Adam had been too late to stop the man from plunging a knife into John's back, but John had taken the murderous bastard with him over the bridge and into the dark, swift waters below. Adam had rushed to the spot where his friend had gone and leapt over the side into the water himself. The fall had nearly killed him, and it had been for naught. He'd searched the water for what felt like an eternity before finally crawling up the bank and collapsing in exhaustion.

As he lay gasping for breath, a man Adam had seen once or twice before at social engagements had emerged from the darkness and rushed to help. That was the night Avery Russell, the man who would become London's new spymaster a year later, had recruited Adam to the Court of Shadows.

After the previous spymaster, Hugo Waverly, died last year, Avery had taken control and restructured the spy network. Many of the older spies had retired, and fresh blood like Adam had been brought deeper into the ring. Adam promised himself he would have his revenge upon John's killers, for as Avery had taught him, French agents worked in pairs, a master and his loyal left hand. Adam did not know which one had perished in the river with John, the master or the left hand, but he would someday find out. Becoming a spy was his penance for being too late to save his friend that night.

A quiet voice broke through Adam's dark thoughts. "Morrey?"

James Fordyce, the Earl of Pembroke, his new brother-in-law, came to his side. He was a fellow member of the private Wicked Earls' Club and had recently married Adam's half sister, Gillian. He and James had a passing acquaintance through their membership in the Wicked Earls' Club. There were only a handful of members he'd been close enough to get to know in the last few years.

Adam hadn't been particularly active in the club or pursuing any rakish wickedness of late. He'd been preoccupied with matters of England's security.

But that didn't mean England had been the only matter on his mind. He'd been searching for his long-lost half sister who'd been working as a lady's maid in London, and that had brought him deeper into James's circle of friendship, for which he was grateful. He trusted the man with his secrets in ways he couldn't trust anyone else.

"Pembroke, good to see you," Adam replied.

James had been the only one to notice him tonight. One of the few who were able to see past Adam's ability to disappear into crowds whenever he wished to.

"Is Caroline with you? Gilly was hoping to see her." A silent question lurked in James's dark eyes, as if he wanted to ask what had Adam on edge.

"No, not tonight." He had convinced his sister Caroline that there would be other balls this week to attend. Once he'd informed her that he had a mission to fulfill tonight, she'd understood the dangers and thankfully had remained home.

"Should Gilly, Letty, and I leave?" Pembroke asked as he and Adam stepped deeper into the shadows at the edge of the ballroom.

"Yes, I would if I were you, but be calm about it—let no one suspect anything. Tonight the *devils* are among us." It was the warning he had devised with Pembroke to let the other man know when danger was close at hand. Pembroke was not a fool. From the time they'd first met, James had sensed that Adam was more than merely a titled lord searching for his long-lost half sister. So without putting James too much at risk, he'd let the man know that he worked for the Home Office in some secretive capacity, though he never went into details unless lives were at stake.

"Right. Well, I see Gillian but not Letty. She must have gone to one of the retiring rooms. I'll go and fetch her."

Adam was only partially listening. He'd caught sight of a woman leaving the ballroom, with another woman upon her arm.

Viscount Edwards's wife, Lady Edwards, the woman he was to protect this evening, was leaving the safety of the ballroom with a dark-haired woman whose face he could not see.

"Find your sister and go, quickly," he said to James before he slid through the crowds now gathering in rows to begin a dance. The pair of women vanished at the doors on the far end, and Adam's fear spiked. Lady Edwards was in grave danger. Her husband had lately been an ambassador to France, and Avery had recruited her to be a spy while she was on the Continent, as he and the Home Office worked in connection with the Foreign Office. She had memorized a verbal cypher that she was to give Avery this very evening, and it was Adam's duty to make sure no one silenced her before she could relay it.

Adam reached the partially open doorway leading out of the ballroom and stepped into a dark corridor. He pressed himself against the wall and moved swiftly from door to door, checking for the presence of Lady Edwards and her unknown companion.

"Hold still. Do not move," a soft, alluring voice said close by. "Be very still, Lady Edwards, lest I prick you. We wouldn't want that."

Christ, he was too late. Some foul French wench likely had a stiletto blade pressed to Lady Edwards's throat.

Adam's hands curled into fists as he moved toward the doorway where he'd last hard the voices. He reached up to undo the first two buttons of his green waistcoat and slid his dagger free. Still concealed by the edge of the doorframe, he drew in slow, steady breaths.

"Be still, I say!" the feminine voice commanded. "I don't wish to hurt you."

Lady Edwards began to beg. "Oh, please, do have mercy on me. I—"

Adam didn't wait another second. He shot around the doorframe and into the room, running straight for the feminine figure in a dark-blue silk ball gown. He caught the woman around her waist with one arm and jerked her back against his chest while he held his dagger to her throat.

"Make a sound and you will not live to regret it," he warned in a harsh whisper. The woman in his arms gasped and went stiff with terror.

"What?" Lady Edwards spun around. Her hands flew to her mouth. "Lord Morrey, what are you doing?" Her blue eyes were wide with fear.

He gave the spy in his hold a tighter squeeze, and she wriggled in his arms. "Saving you, my lady."

"She's not a spy!" Lady Edwards insisted in a frantic whisper.

"She had you at her mercy—I heard her," Adam said.

"Don't be silly. My hair came undone. She was putting the pins back." Lady Edwards held a pair of jeweled hairpins up for him to see. Diamond-studded pins glittered in muted lamplight as the reality of the situation sank in.

He'd made a grave error.

Still holding the woman captive in his arms, Adam slowly lowered the blade. Her breath quickened as though she'd been too afraid to breathe the last few seconds. As he released her, he caught her wrist to keep the woman from fleeing until this matter was settled, and she was sworn to secrecy. She turned to face him, and this time *he* was the one who forgot to breathe.

Letty Fordyce, James's little sister, a beauty he had admired—*desired*—from afar these last few months, was his frightened captive. He released her wrist, and she pulled free. She retreated to the safety of Lady Edwards.

"Lady Leticia," he greeted in a gruff rumble barely above a whisper.

The dark-haired beauty held a hand up to her neck and gazed at him in terror.

"Oh, Letty, I'm so sorry." Lady Edwards grasped the young woman's shoulders and tried to soothe her.

"What . . . ?" Letty stared at him. "Why?"

"We haven't time," Lady Edwards said to her. "Morrey, have you seen Mr. Russell?"

"I haven't. I fear something may have happened to him."

"I must give you the message, then," Lady Edwards murmured.

"No, not me. I am no messenger," he reminded her. "I was only meant to protect you."

He was not one of those spies who played with coded messages and costumes on missions. He was a harbinger of doom, a hand of death for those who tried to harm his country.

"He must be told *tonight*, Morrey," Lady Edwards said.

"What are you talking about?" Letty had finally found her voice. "Why did he hold a knife to my throat?"

"I'm sorry, Letty, dear—not now. We haven't time—"

A creak on the wood floor outside the retiring room made Adam spin around. A pistol barrel, half-illuminated, was aimed straight at them.

He launched himself at the two women, tackling them to the ground.

The crack of the pistol made him flinch as he hit the floor with the women beneath him. A moment later, he rolled off them and leapt to his

146 | MEARA PLATT

feet, blade at the ready, but whoever had fired upon them had fled. He charged into the corridor, seeking any sign of where the assailant had gone.

The crowd in the distant ballroom soon turned to chaos as someone screamed about a pistol being fired. Half a dozen men ran in his direction, and Adam ducked back into the retiring room. Letty seemed to have collected herself and was assisting Lady Edwards up off the floor. Letty was pale, but she wasn't weeping or fainting dead away. She was no wilting rose, and for that he was glad.

"Did you catch them?" Lady Edwards asked as she brushed out the wrinkles in her gown.

He shook his head. "A crowd is gathering, searching for whoever fired that pistol. You must go at once, my lady. We cannot be seen together."

The lady spy nodded and rushed to the open window that led into the gardens outside. Thankfully, they were on the first floor, and Lady Edwards could drop three feet onto the grass outside. She gathered her skirts and slipped through the opening, vanishing into the darkness beyond.

"Godspeed, my lady," Adam said as he closed the window behind her. Then he turned toward Letty.

"Lord Morrey, what—?"

"Lady Leticia, I'm sorry about this."

"About what? What just happened? Why did you hold a knife to my throat?"

"I'm sorry about the fact that I have to kiss you now. I cannot be seen in here alone, not if I wish to avoid being connected to that pistol."

Letty's eyes widened as the sounds of the men in the corridor grew louder. "Why can't you be seen alone? Wait . . . kiss?"

He swept Letty into his arms, holding her tightly to him. And he claimed her parted lips with his. She drew in a shocked breath as he kissed her soundly.

Lord, the woman tasted sweet, too sweet. At any other moment he would have gotten drunk on her kiss. But he kept his focus on the closed door, waiting for the moment it would burst open. When it did, he purposely held Letty a moment too long, making sure the men who'd entered the room saw the girl was quite clearly compromised.

"Good God, it's Morrey!" one man said. Another man called out for Adam to let the girl go.

Adam stepped half a foot back from Letty, his hand still possessively gripping her waist, implying that they had been about to make love. Then he faced the men and dropped his hold on the poor young woman whose reputation he had just put the proverbial bullet through.

"Morrey, what the bloody hell do you think you're doing with my sister?" James demanded. He started toward Adam, vengeance in his eyes that Adam knew would likely end up with his face a bloody mess if this matter was not resolved.

"I . . ." Adam struggled for words as he pushed Letty behind him, keeping her well out of harm's way, lest her brother take a swing at him. He'd given Lady Edwards a chance to escape, but now he was to face an entirely different peril that *he* could not escape.

"We heard a pistol go off," a man said in confusion. Adam recognized him as Jonathan St. Laurent. "We feared something had happened. We thought it came from this room."

"I can't say I heard anything—I was rather preoccupied," Adam said with a rakish grin. He'd become a good actor in the last two years, showing only what he wished and hiding what he needed to.

"That much is clear," Jonathan snorted, his gaze fixed on Adam's chest.

Adam reached up to touch his waistcoat and realized the two buttons he'd undone to free his dagger were still out of their slits. It painted the situation with Letty in an even worse light because it looked as though he'd been in the process of removing his waistcoat.

"We should let Pembroke handle this," another man in the party said. "She is his sister, after all."

"Yes, leave him to me," James growled. "Continue your search."

The other men left the room, leaving James alone with Adam and Letty.

Pembroke closed the door, trapping Adam in the room with him and Letty. "Morrey, what the bloody hell happened?" James demanded, his eyes straying to his sister, who stood nearly silent behind Adam. "I thought you told me to leave because you were up to something dangerous, and then I find you kissing my sister. I expect there to be a damn good explanation for this."

Adam saw the hurt and fury in James's eyes. He had every right to assume the worst. Adam would have, had he been in James's place.

"There is, but I cannot explain here. It may not be safe," Adam replied.

James rubbed his closed eyes with his thumb and forefinger. "You're telling me that what happened tonight was connected to . . . ?"

"Yes." Adam saw that what he was carefully conveying to James was finally sinking in. "And you know what it means for her." He nodded his head toward Letty.

"I know . . . but I can help her weather the scandal. It doesn't have to end the way you expect. I won't force that upon her, not if she doesn't want it."

"Unfortunately, I think you must." Adam kept his tone quiet. "I'm the only one who can protect her. She's been seen, James. Before the night is through, she'll have been made as one of mine, and she will not be safe."

James's eyes widened and then narrowed as he looked between his sister and Adam. Yes, the man was finally coming to understand what Morrey was saying.

"Then we must make a few decisions, mustn't we?"

"We must," Morrey agreed.

"The sooner the better, I suppose?"

"Yes. I'll go to the Doctors' Commons tomorrow. We can tell everyone we had a secret understanding and plan to marry within a few days."

"It will be enough." James sighed heavily. His reluctance to agree to this plan was obviously still strong.

"Wait—marriage?" Letty suddenly seemed to realize what they were speaking about.

"Yes, you and Morrey. Immediately." James glanced at Adam, an apologetic look in his eyes.

"James, you can't—"

"Letty, after what happened tonight, there are reasons that require you to comply with this decision. You know I would never want to force this, but you must trust me. This is the only way forward that keeps you safe."

"Safe? Safe from *him*? This man just held a knife to my throat!"

James shot a startled glare at Adam, renewed worry and anger apparent in his expression. "What?"

"A misunderstanding. I thought she was the threat I'd been sensing. Then the real threat revealed itself and fired. That was the pistol you heard from the ballroom. Whoever took that shot, they saw your sister's face clearly and likely knew that she'd been talking to Lady Edwards."

"Christ." James began to pace the floor of the retiring room. Then he looked at his sister again. "Letty, I've never asked you to obey me for any reason, but that changes tonight. You must trust me now when I say you *will* marry Morrey. All will be explained to you when it's safe."

"James, you cannot ask this of me—please. It isn't fair. You know what I want, and this isn't it." It was such a soft plea, a little sister asking her older brother for his love, his trust, his protection. Adam watched in dread as James had to deny his sister what she needed by a simple shake of his head. No decent brother could form words to deny such a plea, and James was a good brother. All he could do was deny her with his actions.

"Yes, it is unfair," Adam agreed, turning Letty's attention away from her brother. "And for that I'm sorry, Lady Leticia, but it must be done. Do not blame your brother for this. It is my fault. I bear the blame for it."

"No." She shook her head violently. "How can I marry you? I barely know you!"

"Many couples marry knowing each other for less time than we have," Adam said, keeping his tone gentle. It was clear Letty was still in shock. "Pembroke, allow me to have a moment with her."

"I should stay." James's overprotectiveness would have amused him at any other time.

"Just a moment is all I need."

"Very well," James allowed. "But only a moment. My sister has been through enough tonight. I would like to get her safely home before more daggers or pistols come into play." He stepped outside.

Adam grasped Letty's hips again, pulling her toward him. The blue silk of her gown was soft beneath his palms, filling him with desire. Yet she wasn't affected the same way he was. She was trembling, though he could hardly blame her under the circumstances.

"I will explain all that has happened tonight when I can, when it's safe. Please know that I'm sorry for how this came about. I will be a good and loyal husband to you. I swear it upon my life."

Tears gathered in her lovely dark-brown eyes. He reached up and brushed one away.

"Do not cry, please," he begged. "It will be all right. I promise."

Then he stole a soft, lingering kiss from her lips. The sort of kiss he wished he'd given her that first time. She went still in his arms, but not stiff with terror as she had been earlier. He nuzzled her cheek and held her close. The poor innocent creature, barely twenty, a full decade younger than him, was to have her life upended all because she'd sought to help Lady Edwards fix her hair. When he moved his face back to look down at her, all he saw was dazed confusion.

"There, there," he said, his natural need to comfort intensified for this beautiful young woman.

"Do you *wish* to marry me?" she asked him.

"I had no thought to marry. Not in a long while. But I am glad it will be to you." It was the truth. He had abandoned the idea of such things the night John had perished. But now Letty had need of his protection, and this was the only way he could be there to protect her at all hours. He felt like a bastard for having a small flare of happiness that a beauty with such a soft heart would be his. From the moment he'd laid eyes upon her, he'd had a fleeting rebellious thought that she would have made him a wonderful countess. Now she *would* be his countess, and he could not shake his sudden excitement and gratitude at the thought.

"Lord Morrey—" Letty began, but the door opened, and her brother came back inside.

"I have your cloak, Letty. We need to leave. I found Gillian. She's waiting out front." James held up a cream-colored cloak lined with blue silk that matched her blue-and-gold gown. Letty allowed her brother to slip it over her arms, and she buttoned it up with trembling hands.

"Pay a call on us tomorrow, and we'll discuss the ceremony and the matter of Letty's dowry." James held his hat under one arm and nodded brusquely at Adam.

Adam nodded back and watched the pair leave the retiring room. Once he was alone, he searched the chamber until he spotted the small hole in the wall where the bullet had struck. He retrieved his dagger and dug the bullet from the wall. He chipped at the hole, scratching it until it looked like the damage to the wall had been done by something else.

He searched the room until he found a chair about the right height, and then he pushed the tip of the chair into the hole. Now it looked as if someone had simply shoved the chair into the wall at an angle, causing the damage. The last thing he needed was proof of what had happened in this room. He needed London society to think that he simply had been lost in passion with Letty, not thwarting a French assassin.

He slipped the bullet into the tiny pocket of his waistcoat and left the retiring room.

Given the tight crowd now at the front door, Adam surmised that there had been a mad dash upon the poor grooms to fetch coaches and horses. Lord and Lady Allerton were attempting to oversee the mass exodus from their home.

"I don't understand it, Henry," Lady Allerton murmured to her husband. "A pistol? Why would anyone . . ." She trailed off and wrung her hands in her red satin skirts.

Adam slipped between pacing gentlemen and packs of gossiping ladies until he made it to the front of the line. The next groom who rushed up the steps of the Allerton house was breathing hard and caught Adam's summoning wave.

"Bring around my coach. The one with the Morrey crest." He knew all the servants of great households like the Allertons were trained to recognize the crests of the noble houses for occasions such as these.

"Yes, my lord."

Adam moved out of the hot crush of the crowd and waited outside for his coach to be brought forward. He donned his cloak and climbed inside the vehicle once it was in front of the Allerton house. Then he sat back in the darkness for an instant before he realized something was wrong.

He lunged forward, his dagger pressed against the man's throat. He would have laughed in triumph at discovering this hidden man, but he felt a second blade pressed against his own throat.

"Easy, Morrey," a familiar voice chuckled. Adam relaxed, and the weapons were lowered.

"Russell, what the bloody hell are you thinking, sneaking into my coach?" He sat back in his seat and tucked the knife in his waistcoat. Avery Russell did the same. Adam pulled one of the curtains away from the window so that he could better see the spymaster. "Did you find Lady Edwards?"

Avery nodded. "Barely. I saw her escaping from the window after the gunshot. I feared I was too late. We had but a moment to speak in the garden, and I received the message."

"You almost were too late." Adam leaned his head back against the cushioned wall of the coach. "Tonight was a disaster."

"No one was hurt, and Lady Edwards gave me her message," Avery mused.

"No one is hurt, but I'm now to be married."

Avery's eyes widened. "What?"

Adam explained how he'd attacked Letty, and how he'd seen to it that Lady Edwards had the chance to escape safely. Then, to keep suspicion off himself, he'd kissed Letty publicly, making it look as though they'd met for a secret romantic assignation.

Avery fought off a grin. "You're to marry Pembroke's sister?"

"Go ahead and laugh," Adam grumbled.

"I'm not laughing at you, or her. Just the ludicrousness of the situation. Letty is a sweet girl, very intelligent, but not suited to a life of danger," Avery said with more seriousness.

"I know, but what can I do? The spy who fired upon me tonight had a good look at Letty's face. They'll assume she's working with me or Lady Edwards. Pembroke won't be able to guard her as well as I can. She'll be safer being married to me."

Avery was studying him now. "Marriage won't be enough. She'll need you as a protective shadow until we can discover who attacked you at the Allerton ball."

"I plan to be that shadow," Adam agreed. "I only dread knowing Letty will hate me for it."

"I believe Letty is due more credit than you would give her." Avery tapped the roof of the coach with a fist, and it rolled to a stop.

Adam glanced at the darkened street. "You're leaving here?"

"Like you, the shadows are my friends." Avery stepped out into the waiting gloom and soon vanished.

Adam called out to his driver to continue home. He had much to think on and much to plan, including the last thing he'd ever expected to plan— a wedding.

Made in United States
Troutdale, OR
06/07/2024

20402288R00086